CW00502147

1

Other books by Ian Cordery, which are all available from Amazon, in Kindle and Paperback formats.

OUT THERE, SOMEWHERE:

(A collection of 16 Short, Sci-Fi, Horror, Time-Travel and other Stories)

LIFEBLOOD:

(A collection of 20 Short, Sci-Fi, Horror, Ghostly, Historical Fiction and other stories)

SPECTRAL FEAR:

(A collection of 16 Short, Sci-Fi, Horror, Ghostly, Historical Fiction and other stories)

Coming Soon:

INFERUS, THE DARK LANDS:

(The sequel to this book)

The Zone of Light (Extended Version)

By Ian Cordery

THE ZONE OF LIGHT
(Extended Version)

THE ZONE OF LIGHT: (EXTENDED VERSION)

PROLOGUE:

PROLOGUE:

Many moons ago, long before Man lived on Earth; amongst the prehistoric inhabitants of our planet, there began a new species of amphibians; a small life form that became known as the "Dregs".

The Dreg is a Toad-like creature, with a round face and body, they have webbed hands and feet and one missing feature; a Nose! Breathing was achieved through Gill type pores at each side of their necks; which was an advantage to them, as they could live in, or out of water.

The first Dregs were cave dwellers, but they always kept very close to the rivers or oceans. As their population grew, so did their enthusiasm to find adventure, and to seek ways of progression. They had even found a way to live for hundreds of years.

Each day that dawned, bought a new idea to the leading members of the Dreg Clans, until eventually, the Dregs were probably one of the most powerful species on Earth.

Every generation of Dregs developed their skills and knowledge to their best advantage, before passing these down to the youngest members of each clan.

In order to find the strongest and best of these young warriors, a series of dangerous tasks were given to each of them, in order to assess their leadership qualities. And, during the course of these trials, it was also established whether they had the potential to inherit magical powers.

To protect any of their Artefacts, books and everything the Dregs had created or collected over a long period of time, the Elders had found a secret place, to house these objects; a place they named, "The Zone of Light".

A small band of Dregs sought guidance from one of the elders named Hermes, who was the oldest and wisest of the London clan, but due to his ageing years had managed to lose a very valuable book.

Hermes (known to them as the Old Professor) had acquired the ancient Magical manuscripts, when it was handed down to him, from one of the clan elders, who had also warned him of the dangers, should the book fall into the wrong hands.

The enemy of the Dregs were known as the "Jinn", an evil race of warriors. The "Jinn" had heard of the lost ancient Tome and will use every evil method, to get it into their possession, so that they could use it to strengthen their powers; and also, to obliterate the Dreg race!

1: A MEETING OF THE CLAN'S

In a remote part of Snowdon, in Northern Wales, England, a large group of "Toad-like "creatures, which were called dregs, had gathered for a meeting, that would be attended, by the eldest members of all the Welsh dreg clans.

The leader of the main Clan, known as Castor, had called everyone together, to confirm that they will have to relocate, due to the amount of change, which was being carried out, in the surrounding areas of the Snowdon mountains.

Castor was father to only one child, who he had named Hermes.

Hermes was like his father; a bold warrior, but he was also a scholar. He wanted to learn new things every day, and would gather the younger dregs together, on most evenings, to tell them the many stories, that his father had told him, many years ago.

This area of Snowdon, had been inhabited by the dregs for a long, long time, and somewhere, close to the village, lived a dreg elder called Theodore, who was compiling a book.

This book, told the stories of the Dreg Civilisation and would become very valuable for all clans, due to the history, the magical potions and the other things, it contained. Theodore was also a teacher and one of his former pupils, was Hermes, son of Castor.

The dreg clans mainly resided in small, or large caves, or would burrow deep underground; but always close to water, which they could also comfortably live in, due to their amphibious abilities.

Stories had been spoken of, that some dreg communities, had made their homes in the Cities of Cardiff and other largely populated areas of Wales, but these too, were only stories.

The meeting had only just started, and many questions were being fired at Castor; who told everyone to wait until he had finished.

After a long period, it was decided that the elders would send chosen dreg warriors, to search for suitable places, to relocate and that this would be very soon, due to the amount of ongoing activity, around their existing homes in Snowdon.

Hermes asked his father, if he could join the search for new lands, as he wanted to be involved.

Castor agreed to his request and confirmed that Hermes should join his brother, Wadd, who would look after him and make sure he would stay away from danger.

Hermes admired his uncle Wadd. He liked listening to the many stories he told; especially the stories, that some of the dreg elders, had been practising magic.

The following morning, Hermes joined his uncle Wadd and had packed some fruit and vegetables, for their journey.

Wadd had discussed which areas to search, by the elders, and they suggested he should look south.

After a few hours, of both walking and sometimes swimming, they had arrived in a place called Aberystwyth.

Wadd said he had heard of this place and knew that it contained a university, which would be of great interest, to Hermes and also, for some of the younger dregs, who wanted to increase their knowledge.

After several weeks, most of the dreg clans had relocated to different parts of Wales, to start their new lives.

Hermes and his father decided to go to Aberystwyth, mainly due to the recommendations, that his wise brother Wadd had given them, but also, for the benefit of his only son Hermes, who he knew, would spend a lot of his time, inside the libraries, of the university.

The mother of Hermes, Eirene, had moved away a long time ago, after having various disagreements with her partner Castor, over their way of life.

Eirene had gone to join her sister and daughter, Dame, to a place called London.

Dame became interested in the theatre and wanted to learn as much as possible, about the different plays, the musicals, in fact anything that was related to the theatrical environment.

Eventually, as Dame became more independent, she found a suitable place to reside, below the Theatre Royal, in Drury Lane, London.

Hermes had found an easy way to access the library, inside the university of Aberystwyth; he knew exactly where his favourite section was located; the books relating to Magic, illusions and any other associated subjects, that would satisfy his endless search, to increase his ever-growing knowledge.

He had also learned that his old teacher, Theodore, who had lived close to his home, had knowledge of the dark arts, but knew this would only be used in defence, should they encounter any problems or threats, from rival dregs; as, unfortunately, there were a few rogue dregs!

Over the years, Hermes had increased his magical and other skills, to enable him to carry out spells, or to cure minor illnesses, if any of his clan became sick.

He had also, nearly managed to communicate with other dregs, by using what was known as "Telepathy", which astounded his dreg elder teacher, Theodore, who had taken years to perfect these skills.

Hermes had also learned that his old teacher, had been working on the ability to travel through time, and this intrigued him, as he wanted to learn the ways of time-travel, which could be used as an advantage.

Hermes travelled several miles, into the small village, where Theodore lived, and met with some other dregs, who were about the same age as him.

He introduced himself to them and they told him that they'd heard of him, from their village elders.

He met his old teacher, Theodore, who greeted him,

and congratulated him, over the number of different skills, he had managed to learn, in such a short time.

Hermes wanted to learn so much more, from his old teacher, and spent most nights staying there; but returned home regularly, to see his father and friends.

Hermes also wanted to travel further afield, and was planning to find his mother Eirene, in London.

He discussed this with his father, Castor and it was agreed that he would soon leave his village, telling his friends and elders, that he was going in search of more knowledge, in the city of London.

One of his friends from the same village, a young dreg named Cyrus, asked if he could accompany Hermes, on his trip to London, as he had heard of the famous capital and also wanted to go in search of more knowledge, so that he could return one day, and provide for his family.

Hermes agreed and the following day, the two dregs started their journey, which Hermes had confirmed was over 200 miles away, but he had come up with a plan, to ensure they would not have to walk, all the way.

They found their way to the train station in Aberystwyth and boarded the train that would take them to a station in London, known as Paddington.

They hid themselves inside the luggage carriage, in the old steam train and had fortunately, managed to sleep for most of their long journey.

At Paddington station, the two dregs were in awe of the size of the station building, and the amount of train lines, in, and out of it.

Hermes had learned about locomotives and wanted to know more, but for now, they had to find a place to stay, before they went their separate ways, in the big city.

They spent the night, close to a building in Praed Street, not too far from the station, which seemed to be a good idea, as they could smell the different aromas of food; and it *had* been a very long journey.

They fed on the scraps that the humans had thrown into the large bins and rested close by, until the early hours, of the next morning.

The pair were suddenly awoken, by the sound of a large lorry, which was noisily emptying the bins, where they had found some food, earlier.

Hermes spotted a grating close to the bins and they both descended into the drainage channel.

Hermes had seen these gratings before, in Wales, but something told him that they would be a safer way to travel around, rather than be seen by the humans and place them into a dangerous situation.

They made their way through the gulley's and tunnels, then occasionally ascended to the streets above, to get an idea of where they were.

Hermes instincts were gradually beginning to grow stronger, giving him a much better sense of direction.

He asked Cyrus where he wanted to go, and his companion confirmed that he had a brother called Buck, who lived close to a place called Blackfriars.

Hermes accompanied Cyrus through the tunnels and gulley's and after nearly an hour, had found themselves near to a large river, with two bridges, one for trains and the second one, for Automobiles, in the place known as Blackfriars.

Hermes said goodbye to his travelling companion, and hoped they would keep in touch. Cyrus told him he was gradually learning the ways of telepathy, and would make contact, once he was more confident.

Hermes followed his instincts again, and had found his way below the Theatre Royal, in Drury Lane.

He entered the building from the lower depths and could sense that his cousin Dame, was close by.

Dame was surprised at first, but welcomed her cousin Hermes with open arms; as they had not seen each other, for many years.

They spoke of the clans having to relocate to Aberystwyth and of both their mothers, who lived close by.

Dame said she would have to check with her aunt about visiting her, as she had been quite ill recently and wanted to make sure she was well enough to receive any visitors. Hermes understood and said he would speak soon.

Two days later, Hermes returned to the Theatre Royal and hoped that his cousin Dame, had been able to arrange for him, to see his mother.

Eirene, Hermes mother, had been suffering from an illness known as Influenza, which had been quite bad, but she had told Dame that she wanted to see her son.

Hermes greeted his mother with a cuddle and said how happy he was to see her. Dame left them alone and went to get some refreshments.

Hermes told his mother about his father missing her, and about the relocation of the clans.

Eirene started to cough badly; Dame returned and was about to slap her on her back, to relieve the problem, but Hermes had already done that.

He told his mother that he had been learning about different scientific techniques, which included Alchemy, and wanted to bring her some medication, once he could find the right ingredients.

Hermes left his mother and Dame, telling them that he would return shortly, with the medicine.

He collected some herbs and other ingredients, which he had found in a place nearby, called Covent Garden.

He returned to his mother's abode and used a clay cup, to mix and bind the concoction.

Hermes gave his mother a dose of the medicine and she confirmed how refreshing it was, and that she was starting to feel better already.

Eirene had been fully cured of her illness, just two days later and thanked her son for his miracle works.

Hermes was delighted, knowing that what he had learned from the books and his mentor, Theodore, had given him the ability to cure!

Hermes had now fully perfected his telepathic powers and made contact with Cyrus; the friend he had travelled with, from Wales to London.

Cyrus used his thoughts and spoke to Hermes. Hermes congratulated him on being able to finally use the skill and hoped they could meet up soon.

Cyrus told him that he was still staying with his brother Buck, close to the railway station in Blackfriars, and that it would be good for Hermes to meet him.

In Aberystwyth, the dreg clans had gathered for a celebratory feast, to honour Theodore, who had completed the "Dreg book of Civilisation".

Theodore, a dreg elder, and teacher, had compiled his knowledge of all the events he had learned about, over many years. The book also contained many secrets,

17

magical spells and a register of any valuable assets, including talismans, amulets and medicinal cures.

Castor, the father of Hermes, offered Theodore a drink, made from herbs and plants, mixed with water, and noticed that the elderly scholar looked troubled.

Theodore wanted to speak to castor, but now, was not the right time, due to the celebrations, that were in full flow, in the village.

They arranged to meet the following morning, inside the home of Theodore, which was a small cave, close by.

Castor met Theodore, as planned and walked into the bijou cave, belonging to the dreg elder.

They discussed that the completed book was very valuable and contained things that could become a danger to all the dreg clans, should it fall into the wrong hands.

Castor then spoke about an evil race of warriors; Theodore had heard of these evil warriors, known as the Jinn, who lived in a place called Inferus, the dark lands; a place that everyone hoped, they would never have to visit, due to the stories they had been told.

Theodore asked Castor to nominate a place, where his valuable book could be hidden, due to its contents. He also suggested that only chosen elders would be able to access the tome, but only if the clan leaders allowed it.

Castor thought about his only son, Hermes, who he knew, was becoming a proficient master of science and many other skills, and wondered whether the book could be placed in his care, once he had found out where he was living, in London.

Hermes had found a place called The British Museum,

in Russell Square, West Central London. He loved visiting the rooms full of books, and would spend most of his spare time there. On a cold day, early one morning, Hermes left the British Museum, before any of the humans would enter the famous building.

The rain was very heavy and, as he started to make his way to the nearest drain, he saw several people walking very quickly, towards him.

He spotted a basement area and descended the stairs, down to a small yard, to keep out of sight, and noticed an open door.

As the rain showed no signs of stopping, he decided to investigate the interior of the building.

The building was quite old and he noticed that some refurbishment works were being carried out, in the areas, adjacent to an internal staircase.

His intuition told him that the areas below the basement were being excavated.

He entered into an open shaft and used the scaffolding, to descend towards a pit area; which led him into even more spaces.

Hermes had seen enough, he had found a suitable place to make his home; and, being so close to the British Museum, he wanted to move in, immediately.

Over the next few months, Hermes had managed to completely master the art of magic and Alchemy, and with his new, unique skills, had transformed his new abode, into a comfortable residence, with many rooms.

Theodore had been learning about many ways of travelling distance in time, but at the moment, had a lot more work to do, before he could safely use these new skills.

He had waited for Castor to advise him of where Hermes was living, in London, but had not heard from the dreg clan leader, for some time.

He focussed his mind and tried to locate Hermes and heard a voice speak, inside his mind.

He had managed to communicate with Cyrus, who he knew had travelled to London with Hermes and asked whether he knew where Hermes was living.

Cyrus remembered the elder, as his old teacher, and had heard that he was compiling a book about the dreg clans.

Cyrus told Theodore that he had not heard from Hermes for some time and that the last he had heard from him, he was searching for a place to live, somewhere close to a museum, in London.

Cyrus asked Theodore if he could help, and the elder dreg confirmed that he wanted Hermes to look after the book, due to what it contained.

Cyrus wondered whether he could get his hands on this book and told Theodore that he would get back to him soon.

The cunning dreg wanted the book, knowing that it would probably enhance his own, growing powers.

He was going to talk to his brother Buck, but decided not to trouble him over the matter.

Theodore wanted to travel to London, and had thought about his time travelling skills, to transport him. He knew it was a dangerous move, as the equipment he had put together, was made from old parts he'd gathered together, whenever he wandered outside his village.

He knew he was getting older and wondered whether to try out something with the apparatus, but not travelling too far.

He stepped inside a small glass compartment and used his mind to concentrate on moving from inside his home, to the wooded area, approximately 100 yards away.

He turned a small dial and set it to move, for the short distance, but with no change of date, ahead, or behind, the present time.

He pressed a red button and waited. He felt his body tingle and looked at his arms, which slowly disappeared.

Theodore had moved from within his home and was now standing just over 100 yards away from it. He yelled out loudly, knowing that he had nearly perfected the art of time-travelling, but knew he still had a few more adjustments to make, before he could travel further afield, and also, back, or forwards in time.

Hermes had visited his mother a few more times, since she became better and told her, that he was now living close to the British Museum.

Eirene was happy for her only son and said she would visit him soon.

Hermes had been very busy, at his new abode in London; making sure that all his books, maps and charts, were safe, as they were too valuable to lose.

He had made one of his rooms into a sound-proofed area, which he had called, his "secret room". The room would also be used to prevent any of the dreg enemies, from overhearing any conversations, or have access, to any of his valuable articles.

He wanted to invite some friends over, but there was still a lot of work to do, in order to accommodate them, at the moment.

Theodore had finally managed to locate Hermes, by

telepathy, and asked him whether they could meet soon, to discuss something of great importance.

Hermes agreed, but confirmed that he was over 200 miles away and it would take a long time.

Theodore confirmed that he could be with him very quickly and would clarify the details, once he was with him.

Hermes wondered whether Theodore had managed to build his time travelling machine, but then thought about what his old teacher wanted to tell him.

Hermes agreed that Theodore could visit him anytime he wanted too and would await his visit.

A few seconds later, Theodore materialised inside the home of Hermes, which startled the dreg scholar.

'So, my dear teacher, said Hermes, you have successfully managed to build a time travelling device; you must let me know the all the details!'

Theodore explained that his mission was very important and that he'd sensed that the Jinn were starting to learn about his book of dreg civilisation.

Hermes asked him why he had bought him the book. Theodore told Hermes, that he was one of his brightest pupils and could be trusted.

'Together, my dear Hermes, said the old tutor, we will find a place of safety, so that this book, and any other assets, can be safely sent away somewhere, that only us and the dreg elders will know about.'

Hermes was elated; his old teacher had asked him to find a place to hide the items, belonging to the dregs.

He produced some fruit and vegetable and asked Theodore to help himself. Over their light refreshments, Hermes confirmed that he had built a secret room, which was sound-proofed, and would prevent anyone from listening to any conversations.

Theodore was glad he had chosen his old pupil to help him and asked if the book could be hidden, inside this room.

Hermes agreed, and said that the book would be safe inside the room; and asked Theodore to follow him into the secret chamber. The book was placed into an opening, in the rear wall of the secret room, then Hermes secured the aperture, with a large portrait.

Theodore had recently met with some of the elders and told Hermes that they were getting worried about their possessions. He explained to Hermes that various articles had been gathered, over the years and some of these had magical powers.

'The dreg elders, said Theodore, have decided, that they would hide every asset in a safe haven, but nobody could come up with a suitable place.'

Theodore wanted to tell the dreg elders, that he knew of a place, but could not be certain whether it would be safe enough, until they had sent something there first.

Hermes asked if he could assist over this possible venue, and to carry out some tests, to ensure it was safe enough.

Theodore agreed and gave Hermes the coordinates, through telepathy. Hermes could see a very well-lit area, with nothing except a mist within it. His thoughts could not see whether it would be able to support any items, as it looked as though it was just a mass of clouds.

Hermes produced an old broom, then waved his arms. The broom appeared within the mist. It hovered above the smoke, then a very bright glow surrounded the old twig broom.

Theodore witnessed what had happened and asked Hermes to see if he could get the item back.

Hermes waved his arms once more; the bright light disappeared, the mist became thicker, then the broom returned to the secret room.

'Perfect, said Theodore, this is the right place and I will now be able to advise our elders!'

Hermes was ecstatic, he was so proud to have helped his old tutor.

'My dear Hermes, said Theodore, you have witnessed the place where, until now, only I have seen; the place I have named, "The Zone of Light"!'

Theodore congratulated his old pupil for his valuable assistance and said he could now arrange a meeting with some of the dreg elders, in their Welsh village.

Hermes watched as his old teacher and his time-machine, had vanished, but had reminded Theodore, that he was welcome to visit his home, anytime.

2: THE ZONE OF LIGHT

Back home, in Aberystwyth, a meeting of the elders was called by Theodore, who wanted to advise the details of the safe haven, where they could safely send their assets. He also confirmed that with the assistance of one of his old pupils, who was now living in London, that together, they had proved it was a suitable place.

Castor, Hermes father, knew that his only son Hermes was involved and wanted to ask Theodore about him.

Theodore sensed Castor's thoughts and telepathically, confirmed that he was well.

The elders all agreed that their assets would be sent to this new place, which Theodore had named "The Zone of Light", and would start sending their artefacts and other valuables, to this place, immediately!

Cyrus contacted Hermes, and said he would love to meet him soon, as he wanted to learn more, about the magical powers and anything else, that would help him, when he would return to his family, back in Wales.

Hermes said he was happy to help him with his knowledge and invited him over to his home, below the British Museum.

Cyrus arrived at Hermes abode, a few days later; Hermes showed him around his humble abode, but did not show him his secret room.

Hermes sensed that Cyrus had become different somehow and wondered whether he could be trusted.

He had promised Cyrus that he would teach him the magical arts and would honour this commitment.

Over the next six-months, Hermes had decided that his new pupil had learned sufficient skills, but would need to refresh them, now and again.

Hermes learned that Cyrus had returned to Aberystwyth, to his family and that he was able to help them, with any ailments and basic magical spells, whenever they were required.

Theodore visited the village one day and heard that Cyrus had been taught some magical and medicinal skills, by Hermes and wanted to see if he would like to learn any further skills.

Cyrus welcomed the offer from his old teacher, and one day, during a brief lesson in Alchemy, casually asked Theodore about the book of dreg civilisation.

Theodore wondered why he had asked, but thought no more about it; telling him that it was in a safe place, together with some other assets, which only the elders knew of its location.

He continued with the lesson and could feel that Cyrus was trying to enter his mind.

'Why Cyrus, asked Theodore. What is it that you need

to know?'

Cyrus apologised and said that he was having trouble with his telepathy, but Theodore became suspicious.

Cyrus left the class, from the home of Theodore and thanked him for teaching him more skills.

Everyone in the new village were happy that they had moved to a more, quieter area. Their previous homes near Snowdon, had become a conservation area and was much busier these days, so it would have been unsafe, to continue living in constant fear of being found by the humans.

Now that the dreg clan had settled into their new homes, some of the families confirmed to the elders, that they wanted to have children.

Over the next few months, the dreg females started to feel the sense of pregnancy. The dreg males were happy, knowing that their village numbers would increase and that hopefully, their partners would produce a male.

Cyrus was changing; his moods were starting to show to the other members, of the dreg clan. He left the home of his family and found a small place to live, just over a mile from his family's village.

The dregs didn't see a lot of Cyrus after he left, and he then became known as "The Hermit"!

Cyrus was bored, he had magical powers, but had nowhere to use them. He thought about returning to London and, as his boredom increased every day, he started to think about when.

He wanted to have a chat with his old tutor Theodore, before he would leave the village and paid him a visit. He had something on his mind, but would wait until he was "face to face" with Theodore, before discussing it.

Theodore had heard about the moods and behaviour of Cyrus, and when he saw him enter his abode, he wondered what he wanted.

Cyrus looked different, thought the old teacher; his face was wrinkled, as if he wanted an argument!

Theodore greeted Cyrus and asked if he would like some refreshments. Cyrus refused and asked him outright, about the location of the book of dreg civilisation, again.

Theodore told him again, that it was in a safe place and that only the elders knew where it was kept. Theodore hoped that Hermes had still had it secured, inside the compartment, within his secret room.

Cyrus could sense Theodore's thoughts. He now knew that the book had been hidden by Hermes and that it was hidden, somewhere inside his home, below the British Museum.

He didn't want Theodore to know what he was up to, and grabbed him by his throat, then smothered his gills, making it hard for him to breathe.

The old teacher gasped his last breath; he tried to warn Hermes about Cyrus, but couldn't think straight, due to the rogue dreg suffocating him.

Cyrus had fled the village; one of the clan elders had seen him running from the home of Theodore. The elder entered the small abode and saw the body of the old tutor, who was now dead.

The clan elders were called. Castor announced that Cyrus had killed Theodore, but it couldn't be established why!

The clans were upset over the loss of their teacher and started to make arrangements for his farewell from this place.

Castor contacted his son Hermes, to tell him of the demise of his old teacher, Theodore and that Cyrus had been guilty of this.

Hermes wondered why an old friend like Cyrus, had changed from such a mild-mannered dreg, then to become such a cold-hearted killer?

Castor couldn't explain to his son, why Cyrus had carried out the killing, but Hermes had an idea about what his motives were!

'Just be careful my son, said Castor, he may be making his way back to London and he is dangerous!'

Hermes tried to make contact with Buck, the brother of Cyrus, but Buck was not responding to his thoughts. Hermes decided to make the journey, from Russell Square, through the tunnels and gulley's, to the home of Buck, below the underground and railway stations, in Blackfriars.

Buck was surprised to see Hermes, and greeted him with a warm welcome. Hermes told him that he would teach him to understand the powers of telepathic communication, which Buck gratefully accepted, knowing he could then make contact with any of his dreg friends.

Hermes told Buck about the death of Theodore and that it was by the hands of his brother Cyrus. Buck was quite upset over this and asked Hermes if he had any idea of where he was.

'I believe that he may well be on his way to London, said Hermes, as he is trying to locate a valuable book, that was written by the late Theodore!'

Buck asked where the book was hidden, but was told

by Hermes, that it was in a safe place, that only the elders knew of.

Hermes entered the mind of Buck; he spoke to him by telepathy. Within ten minutes, Buck had mastered the communicative art and thanked Hermes for these skills.

Hermes had travelled to Aberystwyth, by the use of his updated version of Theodores time-machine. He had travelled there, to join his father and the dreg clan, for the celebration of the late Theodore.

Theodore's body lay on a hand-made funeral pyre; where the entire clan paid their last respects to the person they knew as a teacher, a professor and a friend.

Hermes bowed before the body and felt unhappy that his old mentor, had not been allowed to live his life, into his later years.

Two of the village elders placed some twigs over the body, laying on the pyre, then everyone bowed their heads, as Hermes waved his arms over the body, causing the twigs to ignite.

After the ceremony, Castor spoke to his son Hermes, and told him that Cyrus needed to be caught, before he committed any further crimes against the dregs.

Hermes knew that Cyrus was keen to find the book of dreg civilisation and wondered if Theodore was murdered, for not telling him where it was.

Castor wondered if Cyrus would hide in the home of Buck, but Hermes told his father that he had recently seen Buck and believed he would not want to be associated with his murdering brother.

'Just be extra vigilant, my son,' said Castor!

Everyone gathered around the ashes of Theodore and spoke of his life and of all the children he had taught the ways of the dreg.

One of the elders asked Hermes, if he would become the new professor and teach the young dregs new skills, but Hermes said he would think about it.

'I would like to be known as the Professor,' muttered Hermes to himself.

Hermes arrived home one morning, below the British Museum, he sensed that he had a visitor, and knew that it was Cyrus.

Hermes saw that Cyrus had been looking for something, judging by the mess, that had been scattered around his, normally tidy rooms.

'What is it you are looking for Cyrus, asked Hermes, and why did you have to kill our friend Theodore?'

Cyrus shouted back at Hermes, stating that he wanted the book of dreg civilisation and, that he was prepared to use force, if he didn't give it to him.

'Then you will have the book Cyrus,' answered Hermes!

Cyrus followed Hermes into his secret room and told him that the book was hidden in a place, that could only be accessed by going through time.

Cyrus asked him how this could be done, but Hermes told him that it was too dangerous and would not risk anyone's life, by revealing the method.

'I want the book now,' shouted Cyrus!

'As you wish, replied Hermes. Firstly, you must enter the cubicle, in front of you; then I will send you to retrieve the book. Once you have it, you must tell me where you want me to send you, as I would rather not see you back in my home!'

Cyrus entered the booth; then Hermes closed his eyes

and waved his hands at the dreg, who was once his friend.

Cyrus disappeared; Hermes had managed to modify the mechanical device, ever since his father had warned him to be extra vigilant.

Cyrus was sent to an unknown place, where he would be held, until the elders decided on his punishment.

Hermes contacted his father, Castor, to confirm that Cyrus was held prisoner in the "Void of Readiness", where he would be kept, until the elders had agreed on his fate.

'Thank you, my son, said Castor, or should I say, the professor, as everyone is calling you now!'

Hermes smiled to himself; he loved his new title.

'I am sorry father, said Hermes. I'm afraid I will not be able to return to Wales, to become a teacher, as I have some very important work to do.'

Castor was not surprised, and knew his son would be working on his magical spells and alchemy, and anything else, that would help others.

The elders had agreed unanimously, that Cyrus would be sent to a place of imprisonment, for at least 100 years, but with occasional reviews, for his crimes, unless anyone would dare, to challenge their verdict.

Cyrus was sent to the "Fortress of Time"; he was alone, and didn't know where he was, and vowed to kill Hermes, if he ever got out of his new prison. He soon found that he was able to move around the fortress freely and would be fed regularly, but would never know who had provided his food and water.

Nine, new born dreg babies had arrived, in the village, near Aberystwyth; each of them was given a name. The first-born male, was named Theodore, in memory of their late, old teacher and professor.

Seven new-born babies, were female, but the ninth was a boy, who was named Alfa, by his father, Brutus.

Brutus had always wanted a son and made sure that his new arrival, would be given access to the best knowledge available, until he was ready to attend classes, with one of the elders, who had now taken over, the position as the village teacher.

Alfa was a keen dreg, he wanted to learn everything, after his father had told him of the stories about the dreg clans, who lived across the four corners of England.

Once Alfa was ready to join the classes, he became a hard-working pupil and would even help his fellow dreg classmates, once the classes were over.

Alfa had heard about the death of Theodore and also, of Hermes, who he admired, and hoped that he would meet the famous professor, one day.

Hermes had agreed with the elders, that any remaining assets, weapons and other artefacts, would now be sent to the Zone of Light, where they could now be safely stored. It was also agreed that only chosen elders could retrieve any articles, subject to the permission of Hermes.

Every item was sent to the safe haven, including the modified time-machine, and Hermes felt that a load had been lifted from his shoulders. His final item was the book of dreg civilisation and, before he sent it, to its new home, he recalled how his old teacher Theodore, had compiled it, to assist the dregs, with knowledge and power, but also, that he had died for it, by the hands, of the rogue dreg, Cyrus!

The book vanished and was now in the Zone of Light. The zone was, as Hermes would say, "In between worlds", where nobody could access, or live.

The dreg clans across England, had heard about the professor Hermes, and wanted their children to be taught, by this wise dreg.

Hermes was happy to help where he could, but said that it would need to be on his terms, as he felt that he would rather stay in London.

It was then agreed that any child, over the age of 20, who wanted to be taught by Hermes, would need to travel to London, so that they could be near the professor. All these new pupils hoped that they would be given regular classes, at the professor's home, below the British Museum.

Hermes was always busy, trying to invent, or adapt articles, that he would find, close to his home. Once they were ready and working, he would store them somewhere inside his abode, but realised he didn't have enough room, should any invited visitors arrive, so he used his magic, to shrink them all, and placed them into a small niche, within his study.

Thirty years had passed, since Hermes had left Wales, to live in London. Over this period, he had become older, but much wiser. He wanted to make sure that his powers would be inherited by a younger dreg, one day, but couldn't think of anyone, that he had tutored, who would be suitable.

He had taught many younger dregs enough powers, to

ensure they were able to live without fear, and also, to ensure that their families were looked after, but he wished he could find someone special, who he could trust and teach, the new skills; and more!

Hermes had heard that his mother was unwell again and went to her home, to see if he could help.

Eirene, his mother, had some respiratory problems, but Hermes couldn't help her this time. Dame, his cousin, who visited her every day, informed Hermes, that she wouldn't last much longer.

Hermes asked his mother, if he could get his father down from Wales, to see if it would cheer her up.

Eirene said it would take far too long, but thanked her son for thinking of her.

Hermes contacted Castor, his father, by telepathy and told him about his partner, and that he could transport him to her home, within seconds.

Castor arrived and was left alone to talk with Eirene. Hermes and Dame made some refreshments, then Castor appeared from the room, with a sad look on his face.

He told Hermes that his mother had passed away, after breathing difficulties, but thankfully, that she had passed away peacefully.

Castor gave his son a small box, which his mother wanted to leave him; it contained a small gold ring. Hermes returned to his mother's room and said his last farewell.

Hermes, his father Castor, Dame and her mother and uncle Wadd were at the funeral of Eirene, which took place in Aberystwyth, where she was placed onto a pyre and set alight, after Castor had spoken a few words.

The elders and the dreg community then joined the ceremony and welcomed Hermes back.

Castor spoke to his son and told him that a young dreg had been wanting to meet him, ever since he had heard about the magic and alchemy he practiced.

Alfa appeared and introduced himself to Hermes. He told him that he would like to become his apprentice; and would welcome any help, with his quest to become a great magician and alchemist.

Hermes looked at Alfa, and sensed, straight away, that this boy was special. 'I will contact you my boy, said Hermes, but first, you will need to come to London.'

Alfa was elated, he had finally managed to fulfil his wishes at last; to be taught the basics of magic, and more, by the old professor.

'Now my boy, said Hermes, we will need to find you a suitable place to live; then I will be able to see if you will be suitable, to learn the ways of magic and other powers!'

Alfa gave the good news, to his parents, to confirm that he had been invited to London. Hermes also spoke to Alfa's father Brutus, and advised him that he would commence the lessons, with his son, once he had found him a suitable home.

One of the elders, who had been appointed to make sure that Cyrus was fed, and in good health every day, during his incarceration, had contacted the other elders, including Hermes, to confirm that Cyrus had served half of his 100-year sentence and that, according to their laws, would need to have his sentence reviewed.

The sole inmate of the Fortress of Time, had not been

a problem, throughout his served time, so the elders were asked to vote on whether Cyrus would serve any further years, in this place, or whether he should be released.

Hermes, who could have been the second victim, of the murderous dreg, following the killing of Theodore, stated that he did not have a problem with the early release of Cyrus, but suggested that he was sent somewhere on earth, where he could be monitored, on a regular basis, until everyone was happy, that he was no longer a threat; Cyrus was released shortly after.

Cyrus was sent to a small village, not too far from Aberystwyth, where he would be given a series of daily chores and would have to prove to the village elders, that he could be trusted again.

One of the elders in the village, who had known Theodore quite well, kept his eye on Cyrus and would have no problem with getting the rogue dreg, back to the Fortress of Time, forever, if he could.

Hermes had successfully trained many new dreg pupils, in suitable venues close to his home; and most of these pupils had either returned to their original villages, or some of them, stayed in London, once they had found a more permanent residence.

Alfa had learned a lot from his mentor Hermes, but he knew it would be a few more years, before he was fully capable, and more confident, with these skills.

Hermes had invited some of the elders to his abode in Russell Square, to celebrate the success of the dreg clans, across the land, who had all been able to settle and live a good life.

Hermes had summoned the dreg book of civilisation,

from the Zone of Light, as most of the elders had never seen it. The book had been spoken about, on many occasions, but nobody, other than Theodore, and Hermes, had seen the words, the diagrams, or any other sections of the book.

Hermes had been drinking some ginger beer, which he had grown to like, and during the spell, to retrieve the book, had somehow managed to lose it.

He tried everything to get the book back, but failed.

He was distraught, and the attending elders wondered how they could trust him, if he couldn't manage to safely get this most important asset back; a book that would prove to be dangerous, if it fell into the wrong hands.

Way below the earth, within a dark and gloomy atmosphere of blue, green and yellow smoke, sat the Supreme Master of the Jinn; a race of evil warriors.

The Supreme Master was named Phobos, who had heard about a lost book, a secret tome which, if it fell into the wrong hands, would spell disaster to the race of people it represented.

Phobos sat on a black throne, which was encrusted with bones and skulls. There were also shrunken heads, which showed extreme fear, on their skinless faces.

Phobos wore black shiny armour, a red cape and a black mask over his entire face, but his red piercing eyes were all you could see of him. His mind was focussed on the missing book, and how he and his evil apostles would be able to get it into their possession.

3: TEA WITH THE PROFESSOR.

A year after the disastrous gathering In Russell Square London, Hermes was still working on ways to find the book, that he had managed to lose.

The old professor sat inside a very small untidy room, which was full of old map's, Ancient Charts and rows of very dusty books, and the remains of the old, time travelling machine, which he had copied from his old teacher Theodore.

'It's Sunday morning and what a glorious day it's going to be, oh, I do enjoy my weekends, now what can I do today? I know, it's about time I invited some friends over for tea later; I can use my Telepathic powers to contact them!'. The old chap muttered to himself.

Hermes always enjoyed having his friends and former pupils over for tea and became excited, at the thought of seeing them once again.

Hermes was one of the Dreg elders and known as the "Knowledgeable" one, or the old professor, or even the old wizard; as he always had his head buried into one or more of his many books.

Over the years, Hermes had learned various "Magical" powers, which were handed down from his dreg Ancestors, but as he was getting older, he was starting to lose some of these.

He knew he would soon have to hand these skills over to someone he could trust; someone who could continue to help others, with these special gifts.

Hermes also considered himself to be a sorcerer, a Clairvoyant and a Master of Astronomy.

'Well, once upon a time maybe', he sighed!

His clothes were simple, hand-sewn rags, which he usually found somewhere in the vicinity of the British Museum.

Today, he wore a long sleeveless waistcoat, a baggy patchwork shirt, brown corduroy trousers and a flat Professors cap, complete with tassel.

Due to having poor eyesight and very bushy eyebrows, he wore "Pince-Nez" glasses, attached to a piece of string tied round his neck, so that he would not lose them.

Just over a year ago, Hermes had invited some dreg elders for a celebration, but, after drinking a few too many glasses of ginger beer, started to perform an illusion, which, due to his tipsy condition, went disastrously wrong.

A book, known as the "Book of Dreg Civilisation", had disappeared during his magical act. The book, which was written by Theodore, the elderly professor, had been given to Hermes, and was sent, for safe keeping, in the "Zone of Light".

Hermes tried numerous ways to retrieve the Book and even consulted all the Dreg leaders, for their assistance, but had no success at all.

The book was temporarily summoned from the "Zone of Light", a secret place where all the magical treasures were kept; and only the elders knew how to access the Zone, to retrieve any items, if there was a problem.

The elders were not happy about the loss of the book, as it had been written a long time ago and everything it contained, the maps, the spells and the Astrological charts, were sacred to each of the clans, but none of their powers could help them locate it.

The book also contained many ancient remedies and secrets, only known to the Elder's; and if it got into the wrong hands, it would be used against them, so it was inevitable, that the book must be found.

The wisest of the Dreg elders insisted that Hermes should appoint a younger Dreg to be taught the Magical powers and skills, to assist him with the return of the lost book, and this nominated Dreg had to be carefully chosen and trained to safely use these powers.

Hermes knew that the wise Elders were unhappy with him, so he had to choose the right person; someone he could trust! The chosen person would then be specially trained with the Magical Arts, and would eventually become a very powerful Dreg.

'Who should I choose, Hermes whispered to himself. Who would be strong enough, wise and trustworthy, who could assist me in undertaking this dangerous quest? I know who would be my choice, but I must make sure that this person is invited along with others to tea later today; so, I had better start contacting a few friends to join me later and they must not suspect anything!'

'I must think carefully', he muttered, then his eyes became heavy and started to close, he fell into a deep sleep and began to dream. **"Zzzzz – Zzzzz"**, the snoring was very loud!

Hermes thought about his apprentice, Alfa during his slumber and started to mumble.

'Alfa will be perfect for this quest, but he is young and other Dregs may not agree with this choice, when they find out!'

The old wizard woke suddenly and looked at his pocket watch, which was held in a gold case. The watch had a luminous face and roman numerals displayed, around a white background.

'Time is moving so quickly he shouted, I must invite my friends over, before it gets too late. I should invite Dombey & Webley, yes, they are good and loyal friends and during tea, I can somehow ask Alfa to assist me with a project, so time to switch on my Telepathic thought's!'

Alfa now lived below a block of offices on The Mall, close to Buckingham Palace. His room was quite small and full of Royal Memorabilia, all of which were collected in, or around the palace grounds.

Alfa knew Hermes very well and had a lot of respect for the old professor, who had taught him so much. Although he was small and timid looking, Alfa was very brave and always looking for excitement.

Alfa regularly invited his Dreg pals to The Mall, as there was always lots of activity in the area. He often dreamt about going on dangerous missions. (Did he have any idea of what was to come?)

Alfa wore a loose-fitting red shirt, with a bootlace tied

around his waist, supporting a pair of "ragged" black knee-length trousers. He also wore "Royal Blue" leggings, but nothing on his webbed feet.

On his head, he wore a denim cap, which was placed over his head, so you could barely see his two large "staring" eyes, and of course, he had no nose.

He had a white silk sash draped across his shoulders, with a turquoise brooch pinned in the centre, which he had also found, in the grounds, at Buckingham Palace.

Hermes was deep in thought and was thinking about what to provide his friends with for tea later that day. Fortunately, he had managed to salvage some fruit and vegetables from a recent visit to one of his favourite places, Covent Garden.

Alfa suddenly felt a strange sensation and knew immediately, it was Hermes, who contacted him by telepathy, which most Dregs had now perfected.

'Alfa my friend, is that you, can you hear me?'

'Yes Hermes, loud and clear, how are you Professor, replied Alfa?'

'Are you free to join me and some friends for tea later, it would be good to catch up with you all. I would also like Dombey and Webley to join us, please tell me you are free?'

Alfa accepted the invitation and agreed to meet everyone, below Russell Square around 4pm.

Alfa confirmed that he would contact everyone and asked if Float and Levi could join them too.

'Of course, my boy,' said the old professor!

Dombey was a large friendly Dreg and very heavy, due to his love of food, his appetite was very big and he would devour anything edible!

His clothing was made from empty potato sacks, and, on his legs, he wore black leggings made from bin liners.

His passion for food was always getting him into trouble, but his great strength was always handy, in the event of any danger.

Dombey was Alfa's best friend and together, they had been on many adventures, since their departure from Aberystwyth, which allowed them to tell numerous stories, about their visits to various venues in London.

Dombey had heard from Alfa, about having tea at the Professors home; Alfa also confirmed that he would be asking Webley, Float and Levi, to join them.

Hermes nearly drifted off again, but chuckled to himself, as could picture a scene where Dombey and Webley, had met Alfa at a sporting venue.

The large green pitch contained a number of human's, who were kicking a round piece of leather.

'What was the game called, he muttered, "Footer", "Sock-ball", I can't remember what Webley called it, never mind, I can ask them later?'

'FOOTBALL, that was what Webley had called it!'

Webley was a very small Dreg and was the youngest of all the London clans. He was actually named Wembley, after the huge Sports Stadium.

He enjoyed living way down below the amazing sports ground and when any games were being played, he always managed to be somewhere else, due to the noisy atmosphere above.

Webley always had a cold that never went away and due to this, he couldn't pronounce the "M", so the name Webley stuck with him.

Because of his ongoing ailment, Webley always

carried a bottle of medicine with him; the contents were the same colour as his large eyes; Red!

He wore a large blue and white scarf, that fully covered his body, leaving only his small webbed feet remaining visible. As his eyes were always "Bloodshot", it gave him a constant gloomy appearance.

'If only Hermes could find a cure for this cold', perhaps I can remind him later' thought Webley.

The old professor sat down on his favourite cosy chair, and suddenly thought about Float, and his strange way of talking.

'What does he call it, "Street-Talk", I think that's it. And Levi, where does he get those strange clothes, he wears?'

Hermes decided not to rest, or he would have fallen asleep again. He moved a portrait on a wall and revealed a small cupboard. He released some fixings and entered into his secret room.

The special room was full of ancient relics, books and maps. He found a padded cushion and returned to his lounge, after securing the doors and the portrait.

He laid the cushion on the floor then waved both his hands over it, and uttered "*MAGIS*"!'

Several more identical cushions appeared; just enough for all his guests later. He then quickly swished his Twig Broom around the floor, and blew the dust away from his books on the shelf.

He also picked up quite a few scraps of paper, each one with an unfinished spell on them, and placed them into a drawer.

'I must complete these spells, one day,' he sighed.

It was close to 4pm and the first to arrive was Float.

Hermes asked him if he would help him, to tidy the rest of the place for him.

'Sho, Prof!' Float replied in his cool manner.

Hermes raised his very bushy eyebrows.

Float was very smart and lived below King's Road in Chelsea; he wore a silk tailored grey jacket and a paisley cravat around his neck. He also wore a black Fedora hat, with a card stating "Press" tucked into a gold band.

'Gets you into the best places' he would answer, if questioned about it!

'I got the vibes Prof', Float exclaimed.

'Oh, the telepathic message from Alfa. can you please speak normally,' asked the old wizard!

'Sure man, sorry, I mean yes Professor!'

Outside, in Russell Square, the pavements were packed with tourists, making their way towards the British Museum, with most of them taking photographs of the Historic place.

Dombey had hidden behind a rubbish bin; he peered over and watched the commotion, then made his way over to a drain close by, which would take him down to meet with his friends.

'Dombey, my good friend', called Alfa.

'Alfa, where did you come from?' Asked Dombey.

'Tell you later my good friend, he replied; but the Professor is expecting us!'

Dombey and Alfa joined the Professor and Float in the room below Russell Square; Float thrust an apple into Dombey's mouth and welcomed everyone.

'Great to see you both, called out Float!'

Levi arrived in Russell Square. He had travelled from his home, below Savile Row, in central London. He was

46

a dapper looking Dreg with lots of character, and looked very smart in his grey wool suit, neatly cut and finished with turn-ups, just above his webbed feet.

He wore a small cap, with a large feather, tucked behind the band, and his cap was half-cocked, to reveal his cheeky looks

He descended into the Professors room below the museum's library, and was greeted by Float.

'Hey, Y'all, it's the Dreg from Savile Row,' shouted Float.

'Wow, Great to see you all', replied Levi!

Hermes asked everyone to be seated and told them there were many things to discuss.

'Firstly, I will get straight to the point of this meeting,' said Hermes.

Everyone looked at each other, with open mouths. '*Meeting?*' they all thought.

'I must inform you all, that what you are about to hear, will involve danger and the possible loss of life, so if you decide to leave after what I tell you, please do so!'

The attending Dreg pals started to stare at each other once again, with their mouths wide open.

'Ahh – Tishooo!'

'Webley, you are late, called out the old professor! Quick, come and be seated, we will fill you in with all the details later!'

'Sorry I am late everyone, I'….

'Never mind, now please sit-down Webley' exclaimed the impatient scholar!

Webley swallowed a large dose of his red medicine, before sitting down.

'Now, please let me have your undivided attention and

do not interrupt, and *please* save any questions for later'; stated the old professor, with a stern gaze at his captive audience.

'You have all, no doubt, heard of the Book of Dreg Civilisation. Well, we, that is I, have managed to lose it!'

'Wow, where', a faint voice cried.

'Never mind now, it is lost!' exclaimed the old professor.

The Professor continued, after the interruption.

'I have now managed to see the lost book in my dreams and can confirm that there are some clues, about the various places we will all need to search!'

'The only clue I can give you at the moment, is that the book is surrounded by a halo, a bright light and in a safe haven. We must find this place as quickly as possible, before it falls into the wrong hands!'

Everyone was silent, for once, as the old professor continued.

'There is one amongst you that will lead the quest; and this chosen one, will soon learn that he has some special powers.'

'Alfa, it is you!'

The dreg friends all looked at the young Alfa, in amazement; as the Professor continued.

'Alfa, you are my choice and I have chosen you, to lead the search for the lost book.'

Alfa looked surprised and wanted to ask a number of questions, but decided to let the Professor finish.

'I will of course Alfa, furnish you with the full details later, but we have more important items to discuss, and we can deal with these, once we are ready to commence the quest.'

'Now, said the old wizard, please help yourselves to some food, then we can continue with the finer details, once we have all eaten.'

The professor sighed with relief, and was happy that he had chosen Alfa.

Alfa wondered why he had been chosen and not one of his other Dreg friends, but then remembered that he had been the apprentice of Hermes, since he'd left his home in Wales.

'Perhaps this is something to do with the strange feelings I have experienced lately?' he thought to himself.

The Dregs all started to eat the feast that Hermes had provided for them, which were salvaged, from below the stalls, in Covent Garden.

Everyone had barely finished their meal and started to fire questions at Hermes.

'All in good time my friends, all in good time, there are many things to be put into place, before we commence our quest, and these will be revealed soon! '

After tea and a few stories, everyone thanked Hermes and said their farewells to all, then the old professor gave them a parting message.

'Alfa will contact you soon, so be prepared for his telepathic call, and I will be there to assist when required.'

'Remember, he continued. Although this will be a dangerous quest, you must never be afraid of what you will come up against!'

Those haunting words seemed to scare the departing friends, but nobody owned up or showed their fears.

Alfa remained seated in silence, until everyone had

left.

'Alfa, I owe you an explanation,' stated Hermes.

'I should have spoken to you before now.'

'No problem, Professor, I have sensed many weird things lately; things I wanted to discuss with you.'

'Yes, my boy, said the old wizard, you are starting to grow stronger and you will find that your full powers will evolve very soon; but we can talk about these in more detail, when the time is right!'

'Firstly Alfa, you must start the quest, by choosing the friends who will be able to assist you; friends who will not fear what they may see; and remember, every stage of the task will be extremely dangerous to you all, so choose wisely!'

Alfa wondered what he was getting into, but he knew the old professor would always be there, to guide him.

'There are evil forces who would do anything to get their hands on our book, stated Hermes. These dark forces will use every trick they can, to get our book into their evil hands, so each one of you will need to be alert, at *all* times!'

Alfa was silent but aware of what was required of him. The professor continued.

'Firstly, in order to begin the quest, you must seek the dreg called Rank, he can be found below the Chelsea Barracks, in the Kings Road, Chelsea, and this is where you must start your journey. Now please go home and get some rest my boy, then you will all be refreshed and ready to commence the search for the lost book.'

'Thank you for everything Professor, said Alfa. I will get some rest later, but will ensure that I stay in touch, at all times.'

'My pleasure Alfa, and I sense that you would like to catch up with your friends; please go and catch up with them!'

'*Alfa!* Hermes shouted, before he reached the exit, to the upper Square. I almost forgot; please take this scroll with you, but do not, I repeat *do not* open it, unless you are in danger!'

Alfa bade farewell to the tired old dreg and made his departure into the square above, where Dombey and Webley were waiting for him.

'You must have sensed I was going to ask you both to assist me in our quest, said Alfa, and I am very grateful for this. Come, let's go and get some rest now, we have a very important day ahead of us!'

The three tired Dregs made their way through the tunnels, below Russell Square and followed the gulley's adjacent to the London Underground tunnels, looking for a safe place to spend the night. They searched for somewhere close to their first venue, which was somewhere near Chelsea Barracks; the place where they would find a Dreg called Rank.

Hermes was sad to see his friends depart, but he knew he would see them all again soon.

'I have a lot to do now the quest has begun, thought Hermes, and I must make sure that all our Dreg friends are made aware and offer assistance, as and when they are required!'

Alfa telepathically confirmed to Hermes that they were making their way towards the Chelsea Barracks ready to meet up with Rank the next day.

'All going to plan so far', Hermes muttered.

4: THE SWORD OF TRUTH.

Alfa loved to travel; his taste for adventure had sent him to many places, sometimes, which were far away from his home in The Mall.

He had no problem with the constant throng of Tourist's above his lodgings, all searching for the famous home of the Queen of England, but he enjoyed getting away from the area, for a bit of "peace and quiet", when he could.

Alfa had been inside Buckingham Palace on many occasions, he loved making his way through all of the large and spacious rooms throughout the magnificent building. (Obviously when there was nobody there and always having to keep out of sight)

He particularly liked the access to the State Room, where he could see a vast amount of magnificent works of Art, Pottery, and a very large set of Elephant Tusks, all adorning the walls and floors, along the endless, red carpeted hallway.

These artefacts, he had heard, were gifts from the leaders, or Ambassadors of the Commonwealth Countries, given to the queen, during their state visits to Buckingham Palace, in South-west London.

The high walls of the long hallway, were adorned with many full-sized paintings; some of which almost covered an entire wall.

Alfa's home in The Mall, was quite bijou, and would be a tight squeeze, to accommodate his two companions, so they decided to spend the night, close to Victoria Railway Station, somewhere below the Underground Station.

Webley looked at the half-empty medicine bottle and looked at Alfa,

'Do you think I will need any more of the mixture?' Asked the small dreg.

Alfa assured him that Hermes would provide some more, whenever he needed it.

Dombey was looking for something to eat, as usual, and glanced at Alfa.

'I am very hungry Alfa', the large dreg exclaimed.

Alfa told him that they needed to make a move and that they could find something to eat, on their way to the King's Road.

It was a Monday morning, and was very busy, at Victoria Station. The Railway and underground trains had transported the human traffic from their homes, in time for them to go to their places of work.

The three chums found their way into the tunnels and gulley's, near Buckingham Palace Road, then made their way below the heavy traffic above, to a place Alfa knew well; an Italian Restaurant, where he knew they could get their breakfast.

Dombey could already smell the food and couldn't wait to savour whatever was on offer!

The Restaurant was already open to the public, who would provide them with coffee, sandwiches and other "take-out" food, to consume at their places of work.

Alfa asked his two friends to wait for a minute, so that he could go and salvage some scraps of food outside the restaurant.

He returned soon after, with boxes of left-over pasta, and various other delicacies.

'Well done, Alfa, Dombey cried, 'I am *so* hungry'!

Both Webley and Alfa managed to grab a few scraps, before Dombey had devoured everything!

After they had finished eating, Alfa confirmed that they should get going.

The three Dregs made their way back to the tunnels and gulley's below Victoria Coach Station and advanced towards Sloane Square.

'We're quite close to the big River, Alfa confirmed. It will be quicker if we make our way to Chelsea Barracks along an underground stream close by, so get ready to follow me!'

Alfa produced a small piece of cord from his pocket. He tied it round his waist and connected it to the others.

They all descended deeper into the tunnel and soon heard the sound of water rushing by.

Alfa tugged the cord twice and pointed upwards.

'We are close to where Rank lives', confirmed Alfa.

Their ascent led to another tunnel, where he unhitched the cord from his companions and asked them to wait for a while, as he felt that he was being contacted.

'Hermes is trying to contact me he cried; can you please give me a few minutes and I will find out what he wants and whether it is important, or about our meeting with Rank!'

The young dreg climbed up towards the busy King's Road, then spotted a tunnel by a drainage gulley, which would allow him to concentrate and receive the telepathic message from Hermes.

'I hear you professor, what can I do for you?'

Hermes responded and asked his young pupil to focus on a shape that would soon appear.

Alfa could see a Pentacle and as he looked into the shape, he heard Hermes speaking to him.

'Listen carefully to what I am about to say, asked the professor. It is very important, so please concentrate on the Pentacle, and let me know what you can see?'

'I can see some letters and symbols, replied Alfa, I can also see beyond the talisman, but what does this mean?'

'Your powers are getting stronger my boy, and you will need to be ready to use these against the Dark Forces, when required!'

Alfa started to shake with fear, but his mind remained focussed.

'You are about to commence your quest and this will involve solving many clues, said the old professor. These clues may not be easy to solve, but you must think carefully, or contact me, so that you can be sure, you have the correct answers!'

Just then Alfa heard a strange noise – **Whoosh**!

It broke his concentration so he called out to Hermes, but a strange voice started to echo in the tunnel, a voice that spoke in a threatening way.

"You will not find the Book you seek. You will fail in your quest; we are more powerful than the Dregs!"

Then the Pentacle disappeared!

Alfa could clearly see two large "Orange" piercing eyes in its place, then the voice continued.

'We are the Jinn; we are the Masters on this earth and we intend to find your lost book and destroy the Dregs forever!'

Alfa wondered about what the voice had just said, and knew that they would need to be on their guard, at all times.

The eerie voice spoke again.

'Should you and your two feeble friends proceed with your search, you must be prepared to accept the consequences!'

The echoes of the harsh message pounded into Alfa's mind.

'I will not be afraid, he shouted, I must continue the search for the sake of our people, I will not stop now!'

Hermes spoke once more.

'That was your first encounter with Malus, known as the "Prince of Curses". Exclaimed Hermes. Malus and his evil warriors are known as the "Jinn" and they will do everything they can, to get the book for themselves; but we must continue our quest, so that we can get our book safely back!'

Alfa was slightly shaken, after Hermes had explained who had just spoken, but confirmed to him that he would not allow anything or anyone to stop the quest, to achieve their goal.

'Alfa, Alfa, where are you?' called Dombey.

Dombey and Webley had become impatient and wanted to move on.

'What is going on, did Hermes contact you, are we ready to move on, asked the large dreg?'

'So many questions Dombey, we must all be patient, and we need to find Rank, as soon as possible!'

Alfa did not want to discuss his encounter with Malus; as he didn't want to scare his friends, or be bombarded with *any* further questions

Hermes spoke again.

'Before we were so rudely interrupted earlier in the tunnel Alfa, I have further news for you.'

'There is a sword which will assist you, if you need it. This is a very powerful weapon and will only work, when it is held by a dreg!'

'A weapon, thought Alfa, now that sounds promising!'

'This special blade, continued the old wizard, is called "The Sword of Truth", and can be summoned to assist you, but only, if you are in any danger.'

Alfa thanked his master, for the good news and called his aides to complete their journey to the Chelsea Barracks.

The three Dregs found their way to the Barracks and ascended to the upper level, where they could hear some shouting and what sounded like feet stamping on the ground.

'There, look, shouted Dombey, look over there, who are all those people?'

The three pals were hidden behind a large tree and looked across the grounds of the barracks, to see what was happening.

'Left, Right, Attention, about turn!'

These orders were directed to a squad of 20 or more Veteran human soldiers, who had formed 4 rows of equal distance, once they had heard the command.

Dombey gazed in awe at the elderly troops, he had never seen such precision.

Webley asked how they were going to find Rank, with all the commotion that was going on.

'I am sure my instincts will tell me,' thought Alfa.

Rank was a very old friend of Hermes, he was one of the elders, a wise old Dreg but not well liked by some of his clan, due to his constant salvo of orders to everyone.

Rank always dreamt of having a Dreg Regiment under his command, but it was just a dream.

He wore a red tunic, neatly cut below the waist. His navy-blue trousers were neatly pressed and had a thin red stripe on each side. Also, he wore a shiny leather black belt to support these well-cut trousers. There were three white stripes on his tunic, as Rank decided he wanted to be a Sergeant.

Every morning, he made sure he was awake before the sound of a Bugle, so that he could watch the troops.

After breakfast in his small room below the barracks, which he had named "The Mess", he spent most of the day dreaming of this proposed "Secret Army", an elite band of dregs, that would assist his colleagues when required.

The regimental dreg had tried many times to convince the elders of his military plans, but as always, nobody wanted to get involved.

Rank wished that his dreg friends would pay him a visit now and again, as he missed what was going on beyond the barracks, but he felt his place was to stay on site, in case he was asked to recruit any willing Dregs, for his proposed "Secret Army".

Alfa could hear these thoughts; his mind was now focussed, onto the regimental dregs position.

Rank sensed that someone was near; had someone come to visit him at long last?

'Hermes is that you,' asked the old soldier?

'No Rank, my name is Alfa and I have two friends with me; and we are close by.'

Rank picked up his red cap with a black shiny peak, placed it neatly onto his head and dusted himself down as if ready for inspection, then made his way over to the King's Road edge of the Barracks, via a secret foot tunnel.

'Welcome all of you, I am Rank, how can I help? '

All three Dregs gave Rank a military salute, it seemed to be the natural thing to do, owing to the way he was smartly dressed in his Military attire.

'Thank you for the salute, everyone, it is very good to see you all!'

'I was just thinking about Hermes said Rank, and was hoping he would be coming to see me, but you all arrived, how exciting about this quest. Please follow me to my humble abode, I will make us some lunch.'

Dombey was going to ask about eating, but Rank had already spoken the magic words.

Alfa and his friends followed Rank through a tunnel, and into a small, but very tidy room.

They were seated on small stools, around a circular makeshift table, where some snacks had been placed under serviettes, as if he knew they were coming?

During lunch, the conversation initially started with the mention of the quest and what he could do to help, but the discussions soon drifted into Rank's visions of his "Secret Army" and how he had constantly asked the elders to agree with him.

Alfa stated that the quest was of paramount importance, and that they could discuss any other points very soon.

Dombey and Webley discreetly helped themselves to some food and asked Rank about the many medals, they had both spotted, on the surrounding walls.

'My friends, cried Alfa, we need to advise Rank over the quest to find the lost Book of Dregs and we have much to discuss! '

Rank looked at Alfa and thought to himself, how brave this young boy is, he would be a perfect candidate for his Secret Army!

Rank explained that he was with Hermes and the elders, when the book suddenly disappeared.

'Everyone assumed that he was performing an illusion, but then, stated the smart soldier, the book suddenly vanished?'

Alfa looked at the concentration on both Dombey and Webley's faces and knew they were the right dregs to assist him, with the first part of the quest.

'I seem to remember at the time, stated Rank, that Hermes had been discussing one of his favourite hobbies, Trains!'

Rank searched his memory banks, to see if he could offer his guests any idea of where to commence their pursuit.

Rank drifted into his deep thoughts, with his

"Tactical" mind working overtime.

'The place you seek, said Rank, is called the "Pleasure Gardens", which you will find, within a place called Battersea Park.'

Alfa seemed to recall this place called Battersea Park, from stories told, by the old professor, but continued to listen carefully to Rank.

'Here, in this park, said Rank, you should search for some old abandoned Railway tracks that Hermes used to visit regularly. These tracks are hidden now, but if you look very carefully, you should be able to see them.' Dombey couldn't imagine the old professor being interested in trains and smiled to himself.

'Follow the tracks until you find the spot where the old 'Tree-Walk' used to be, continued Rank. You will know when you are in the right place, as there will be two large trees opposite each other; one on either side of the road.'

'These Trees, Rank confirmed, were used to support a platform above the ground, a raised path that used to convey the humans across to the old Funfair.'

After finishing the food that the Sergeant had provided, he spoke again, to his new Dreg friends.

'I would come with you all, but I must stay here, in case the elders contact me about my Secret Army, you do understand, don't you?'

'We must be on our way Rank, said Alfa, and thank you for your kind hospitality and valuable help.'

'We *will* meet again soon', Alfa promised.

'I do hope so,' replied the old soldier.

By telepathy and during their route to Battersea Park, Hermes had told Alfa more about the old railway, that

Rank had spoken of.

'You will need to search above ground this time,' explained Hermes, 'but you must *not* be seen by the humans!'

'Also, the railway and the tree walk are no longer there, so you must all follow your instincts.'

Hermes was silent for a short while, but then explained why to Alfa.

'A long, long time ago, I buried something close to the old Railway, and near the Tree-walk, but my memory is failing me, oh what was it. Was it a Talisman, or a chart.' he muttered?

'*Eureka*' he eventually cried!

'It was a Map Alfa, a Map of an area called Mayfair, which contained details of some unknown access tunnels, below Park Lane.'

Alfa made a mental note of the details, in his ever-growing memory bank.

They made their way via the Barrack Tunnels, toward the big river, the river Thames and the many tunnels below it; way, way down.

The trio of adventurers found some new tunnels and could sense the large flowing river above them.

Alfa thought about the comments Hermes had sent him, regarding the possible location of the Mayfair map and his sense of direction took them from the tunnels under the river Thames, then up to the grassy area and tree-lined paths of Battersea Park. It was a very sunny day, and there were three shadows, cast beneath the vast number of large trees, at the side of the pathways.

'Look, here are some old Railway tracks!' shouted Alfa.

Dombey and Webley now accepted Alfa's extraordinary perceptions, and no longer questioned how or why he could see things that they could not.

Two faint lines were slightly visible on the grass when the sun shone over it, between the paths and the trees, which they followed very carefully.

Eventually, Alfa pointed at a large tree on the opposite side of the road, which was in line with a tree on their side of the road. He then thought about the Tree walk platform, as mentioned by Hermes.

'Here, Alfa called, we have found the place we must commence our search for the Map, so we must dig quite close to these tracks!'

They each found a sharp stone, or a stick, and started to dig, in close proximity to the tracks.

After several minutes, Dombey suddenly called out, stating that he had found a dull looking, long metal box, which he passed over to Alfa.

'Well done my good friend, said Alfa, this will hopefully be the Map?'

Alfa opened the box and saw a long scroll inside, so he closed it, to keep it safe.

He pointed to an opening close by, and asked his two companions to accompany him into the small aperture, close to the river's edge, just below some railings and a wall.

Once inside, Alfa unravelled the scroll and they saw the Map which clearly stated, *"Park Lane, Mayfair"*.

Upon closer inspection, he noticed several buildings highlighted on the chart., but then sensed they were being watched.

'I feel we have company, Alfa whispered. We are

being watched, so do as I say please!'

'Quickly, we must join hands, said Alfa; no questions, just do it!'

As soon as they had connected, they found themselves outside the small aperture.

They looked around and saw that the buried Railway Tracks were now evident above the grass and also, above them, was a timber platform with wooden stairs for access, on either side of the road. They had gone back in time!

They looked along the old railway tracks, to see if there was a train, when suddenly an eerie voice boomed out loud.

'You cannot hide from me'! which seemed to come from the Tree walk platform above them.

All three Dregs looked up and spotted a dark black cloak and an evil looking spectre, with two piercing orange eyes!

The wooden platform started to sway, softly at first, but then a strong gale forced the platform to move more violently.

Alfa stared at the evil presence and gulped; he remembered seeing the two orange piercing eyes before, in a vision, when they were in the tunnels, adjacent to Kings Road and Sloane Square.

'Crack!'

A bright green flash hit one of the railway tracks by Webley.

'Crash! **'Crack!'** two more bolts of green lightning struck the rails; then the eerie voice spoke again.

'You will obey my commands; and you will give me the Map!'

Alfa took a deep breath and spoke.

'No, I will not give you the Map and beware, we are armed'!

'Crack, Crack'! Two more lightning bolts hit a tree, close to where Dombey was standing.

'Give me the chart!' Asked Malus once again.

'The Sword of Truth, I must summon the Sword,' Alfa *whispered.*

He raised his webbed hands toward the sky, a blue halo appeared and, in its centre, was a bright, shiny blade.

He used his powers to summon the Sword from the hazy mass.

He then gripped the weapon with his right hand and gestured to the shadow on the Tree walk.

'Now we shall fight Jinn!'

Alfa climbed the access stairs two at a time, up to the platform.

Crack, crack, thud!

A lightning flash caught the tip of the blade, making the Sword glow brightly.

'Be warned evil warrior, shouted Alfa, *this sword is too powerful for the Jinn!'*

The two orange eyes burned with anger.

Alfa made a circle with his left hand around the evil shadow, then a circular misty glow formed around it.

He then pointed the Sword at the circle and everything, including the Jinn master, disappeared. Everything was gone except for the smoky mist.

From the mist, the dregs heard a loud laughing voice, which made them shiver.

'We will meet again oh little ones, you have

succeeded this time, but you will not beat me next time!'

The sun was shining once more, the three companions had returned to the present day.

The Tree-walk and the railway tracks had disappeared.

'Phew, I thought we were in trouble then chaps,' Alfa declared.

He consoled his terrified colleagues and told them that the sword had saved them, and that no doubt, there would be more clashes with this evil enemy.

'Where is the sword' Dombey asked. Alfa confirmed that it had been returned to its home and could be called back, whenever it was needed.

Alfa further explained that the dregs had a vast arsenal of weapons, which were kept safely, in a place known as "The "Zone of Light".

Alfa suggested to his weary friends, that they should look for somewhere safe, to rest and think about what they would need to do next.

Alfa looked around and could see that they were very close to a large building, with four, very large white pillars.

'This, my friends said Alfa, is Battersea Power Station, and we should find somewhere below this place, to rest for the night. I think we've had enough excitement for one day, and we must regain our strength, so that we can continue with the next stage of our quest, tomorrow.'

Dombey stated that he was hungry again. Webley gulped a large dose of his medicine.

'Let's sleep first my friends, we can find somewhere to eat a bit later,' suggested Alfa.

As the tired duo slept, Alfa wanted to study the Map of Mayfair in closer detail. He saw two crosses on the chart; one marked the position of a hotel.

'The Dorchester Hotel,' he whispered!

The second cross was marked over a building, close to the hotel, but he was unable to establish its name.

'Oh well, Hermes will be able to explain,' he whispered.

Alfa looked even more closely at the map; he saw something scribbled close to the two crosses. There was a faint arrow just below the cross by the hotel, which pointed to some words. ***"Snak lives here"****!*

Alfa remembered Hermes talking about Snak many times, when telling him about some of his adventures.

The brave Dreg was feeling tired and, as he started to drift into sleep, the map, together with its container, suddenly disappeared.

'I will sleep better tonight', Hermes mumbled. He had transported the map to his secret chamber.

'Good boy Alfa, you did well today. Tomorrow, you will find Snak in Park Lane, close to the Dorchester Hotel; now sleep well, my Dreg friends.'

Alfa could hear these words in his sleep.

5: AN EVIL HORSEMAN IN PARK LANE.

The four identical pillars of Battersea Power Station, gave an eerie feeling to Alfa, as he visually surveyed the area, they'd stayed, the night before.

The noise of the humans driving their vehicles toward to bridge was very loud; confirming that "Rush-hour" was now in full flow.

"Peep-Peep, Honk-Honk"!

The impatient humans wished they'd left home five minutes earlier; hence the perpetual sound of their hooters, which made Alfa chuckle too himself.

Dombey had started to wake up; Webley yawned and opened his medicine bottle and gulped a large dose. (Webley hadn't noticed that Hermes had replenished the medicine, while he was asleep)

'Has anyone seen the map', cried Alfa?

Hermes voice was then heard by the three comrades.

'The map has been destroyed Alfa, due to the interest by the Jinn so I trust you have memorised the contents.'

Alfa confirmed that he *had* memorised the entire map and in particular, the Dorchester Hotel and surrounding buildings.

Hermes explained that the building, close to the Hotel, was an underground Library and that Snak, will be able to assist you all, once you meet him.

'What is the significance of Park Lane asked Alfa; and what is it we are searching for?'

'All in good time my boy, all in good time!'

Hermes explained that Snak would be able to guide them through the library, where he would help them to find an old Almanac, a book which would assist them with the next step of their quest.

'Snak knows this place very well, explained Hermes, and please be guided by him.'

Alfa couldn't wait to see Snak, he'd heard about him from Hermes, on many occasions.

'You must all be extra vigilant during your search for this Almanac, continued Hermes. Malus, was not amused by the incident at Battersea Park and he will, no doubt use his evil magic, to ensure he can defeat you all, next time!'

Dombey and Webley were asked to return home by Hermes, so that they could rest after their recent events. He also asked them to be ready to assist Alfa, whenever he needed their help.

They both wanted to continue with the quest and stated that they hardly did anything at Battersea Park, but Hermes insisted that they would be more helpful once they had properly rested.

After the pair had said their farewells, they departed the Power Station and headed for the nearest drains and gulley's, to take them back home.

Alfa made contact with his two friends, Float and Levi and asked them to meet him at Hyde Park Corner, later that day.

He suddenly shivered, after recalling the events of the previous day and wondered what was in store, in the library, at Park Lane.

Deep down, in the lower depths of the Earth, a meeting was being held. A meeting of the evil Jinn forces, which was hosted by Malus, who was seated on a large, odd-looking throne.

The throne was made of old bones, skulls and many teeth, all encrusted over the back and sides.

Malus was joined by four of his evil Jinn disciples; Belua, Kalor, Tavet and Asper.

'We must find out where the Dregs will surface next, bellowed Malus*, we must foil any attempts they make to succeed with their quest, and we must destroy the entire dreg civilisation, whatever the cost!'*

Malus continued speaking to his attentive evil henchmen, who would not dare to interrupt.

'They managed to produce a magic sword when I journeyed back in time, to the park, but it somehow disappeared before I could steal it from them! We must not assume that these young warriors are easy to defeat. One of them, their young leader named Alfa, appears to have power's that I have not experienced before?'

The four evil Jinn warriors sat in silence, and listened intently, when their master spoke again.

'The other Dregs who were with the boy, were not a

threat and only there to assist, but we will need to use
our evil strength together and defeat them all, whatever
the consequences!'

Hermes sensed that the Jinn were planning a
"Counter-Attack" and wanted to warn Alfa, before his
young apprentice began his search for the Almanac.

Alfa was resting in a tunnel close to Knightsbridge,
when Hermes made contact. The old wizard warned him
that the Jinn would probably try and prevent him, from
getting the Almanac at the library.

'You have already encountered Malus, the Prince of
Curses, stated the old professor, but he rarely makes an
appearance, and would normally send one or two of his
evil henchmen to confront any foes. Also, he has several
followers, each one having special "Dark-Magic"
powers, which were used for evil against anyone, who
would dare, to try to and stop them!'

Hermes had a brief description of the Jinn followers,
as written by the Elders and confirmed these to Alfa, so
that he would be able to identify each of them, by their
appearance and evil skills.

Hermes started to confirm the details of each of the
Jinn warriors.

'The first on my list is Belua; next to Malus, Belua
was probably the evillest Jinn soldier. He has the power
to create illusions; visions that were so horrible, the fear
would leave any person paralysed, and he can be
recognised by his scarlet armour and black cape!'

Alfa noted these details very carefully.

'The next one is Kalor,' continued the old wizard.
Kalor can command any object to vanish, or to turn it

into stone. He wears green armour, a blue cape and sometimes carries a large sword, with a skull on its handle tip!'

Alfa shuddered at the thought of these different evil powers, which, once again, he saved in his memory.

Hermes continued with the descriptions.

'Next there is Tavet, who rides a fire-breathing black stallion. Tavet has black armour, a white cape and carries a lance. He is probably the most feared Jinn warrior, as he could command ferocious animals to assist him when required and also, he is surrounded by a ring of fire.

Hermes shuddered at the thought of his first meeting with Tavet, and tried to clear his mind about it.

'Finally, there is Asper, who is known as "The silent one". Asper's methods are also very frightening, as you will not be able to hear or see him; he can assume many shapes or forms and beware, his eyes are lethal!'

Hermes warned Alfa to make sure that he, or anybody with him, was not to look into Aspers eyes!

'Please heed my words Alfa, I know that the quest to retrieve the book of dregs is not an easy one, but remember, you can call on the "Sword of Truth", or other magical items that we can talk about, depending on who, or what you are up against! And, as always, my boy, you may call any of your friends, to assist you, when you need them.'

The four descriptions of the evils Jinn warriors, were memorised by Alfa, and he asked Hermes if there were any others to worry about.

The old wizard recalled that other Jinn warriors were encountered by his ancestors, many years ago and related the story to his young apprentice.

'The elders fought a long battle, which resulted in many losses on both sides. Also, if any of the Jinn soldiers failed to succeed with their mission, they were banished to a place of punishment for their failure.'

This place is known as "The Bastille of Pain"!'

'Sounds very painful,' thought the young apprentice.

'Many Jinn soldiers were sent to this evil place, due to their failure, continued the old wizard; how many was unknown, but better they were confined there, rather than here!'

'Has any of the Jinn ever escaped from this evil place Professor?' Alfa enquired.

Hermes thought about many battles he had been involved in, against the Jinn, then replied to Alfa.

'A soldier of the Jinn army, had managed to escape the Bastille of Pain, wanting to atone for his failure. His sole aim was to destroy the dreg population, and his name was Zaleth!'

Hermes remembered he had encountered the evil Jinn, Zaleth, which made him shiver!

'Zaleth gathered a small army of Jinn soldiers, continued the old wizard, and I, together with some younger Dregs, were sent to confront them!'

(Alfa couldn't visualise Hermes being a Dreg warrior)

'Nearly all the Dreg warriors were defeated, but my teacher at the time, Theodore, summoned the "Sword of Truth", from the Zone of Light, which gave us the upper hand, due to its magical powers.'

Alfa recalled the stories of the dreg Theodore, who had written the lost book.

'Zaleth was killed by the sword and the remaining members of his disciples retreated swiftly after.'

The old professor wanted to say more, but for now, would keep some of the details to himself!

'We must try and forget the past my boy, said Hermes, but remember, the Jinn Disciples of today, are twice as cunning! Oh, and just one final matter to consider Alfa, Zaleth was the *brother* of Malus!'

Alfa thought about his Master's comments and accepted that further dangers lay ahead, however; his strength and growing powers gave him more courage, so he decided to take everything, as it came along.

He asked Hermes to send him any other details, which would confirm whether the Jinn had any weaknesses.

A Dossier soon appeared in Alfas webbed hand, he read the details, and made the papers disintegrate.

Levi and Float had already found their way to Hyde Park Corner and couldn't wait to see their friend Alfa.

Float was a cheeky type and would sometimes end up in trouble for his conduct, but he would tackle any problem, no matter what!

Levi was also a good ally and, like Float he enjoyed any dangerous experiences.

Hermes had told Alfa that Levi had a wealth of knowledge in Science and History, which would be valuable to them all, in their search for the Almanac.

Speakers Corner in Hyde Park, was a very busy venue. There were crowds of human tourists, from all over the world, listening to the various narrators "airing" their views of subjects to anyone who would, or wouldn't listen to them.

Levi and Float had already made their way to the location in Park Lane and were suddenly interrupted.

'Good day my friends'! Alfa called out to them.

'How, where, what' the two Dreg friends called out.

'Good to see you both; I will explain everything to you later, replied Alfa, as we have a very important mission to carry out!'

'Now, said Alfa, we have to find a Dreg called Snak; he will be able to show us where to look for an Almanac, so let's begin!'

After a quick briefing, the trio of Dreg pals descended into the nearest drain grating and, within several minutes, found their way below the large, and very busy Dorchester Hotel.

'I sense that Snak is nearby, stated Alfa, so if you two can find a suitable place to sit down and discuss our "Plan of Action", we will meet you there shortly!'

Alfa had no idea what Snak looked like, Hermes only gave him a brief description and he assumed that he was looking for a very large, overweight Dreg, but how wrong he was!

Snak lived below the kitchens of the Dorchester Hotel; he was an eccentric type, and was sometimes described as a "Toff". He was quite thin, and very agile, nothing like the description Hermes had given, to Alfa.

He wore an old dinner suit, which had seen better days, a black bow tie and a black beret. He ate most of the scraps that came from the Hotel Kitchen, so he ate well.

Snak was busy collecting some food, as his rations were getting low and he failed to notice the small dreg behind him.

'Hello, you must be Snak' Alfa called.

'Good morning my dear Alfa, Hermes told me you were coming to Park Lane, how are you?'

Snak asked Alfa to follow him back to his abode, so that he could store his newly found supplies.

'Float and Levi are close by Snak, said Alfa; so, let's drop off the food and we can then look for them.'

Snak put away some of the items, but quickly wrapped up a few scraps of food, assuming that everyone would be hungry at some stage.

They found Float and Levi close by; Snak introduced himself to them, and removed his beret, as a mark of respect.

Alfa asked everyone to sit, then briefly spoke of the map of Mayfair.

He confirmed that there was a library close by, where they would need to search for an old Almanac.

The only clues, once they had reached the library, was that they would need to access several long tunnels, which would eventually lead to the correct location.

Snak was delighted to be part of the adventure, it had been a long time since he'd had any excitement.

Snak opened up a piece of cloth and shared out some food for his friends, explaining it would give them more strength to assist their search.

While everyone was eating their lunch, Snak produced a silver box and explained that Hermes had called it a "Talisman", asking him to carry it with him, during the mission, in case it was needed.

'I can see the quizzical looks on your faces, said Snak, but Hermes specifically requested that it should not be opened, unless there was a dangerous situation!'

'Come on everyone, said Alfa. We must get going, as we need to search for the long tunnels, as soon as possible!'

Alfa needed to motivate everyone, but he had butterflies in his stomach, not knowing what they would find ahead, or whether they would be joined by the evil Jinn forces, again.

Alfa's instincts, which were quickly becoming accepted, lead them through some long tunnels, to a building in Mount Street, close to Park Lane.

They followed these tunnels, but eventually came to a dead-end.

Snak suddenly had a strange feeling in his stomach and gripped the "Talisman" very tightly.

Float pointed to a large timber door, a door that looked out of place. The door contained four square panels, each having an animal carved onto it.

Levi examined the timber door and referred to the animals carved into the panels.

'Look, there is a Goat, a Fox, a Dog and a Horse, what does this mean?'

He didn't get a response.

Alfa sensed that danger was close by and although Snak had a Talisman, he remembered to bring the scroll that Hermes gave him, just before he left Russell Square. He checked and could feel that the scroll was safely hidden under his shirt.

Alfa concentrated on the timber door and realised he could actually see through it.

He could see a spiral staircase the other side and asked his colleagues to join him before they went through.

'Everyone, called Alfa, please join hands!'

The four of them immediately found themselves at the top of the spiral staircase.

Everyone followed Alfa and made their way down the

winding staircase, each of them looking round and making sure that they were alone.

After reaching the bottom, they spotted a long corridor, but there was no lighting.

Alfa magically produced a rod, then tore off a strip of his shirt; he wrapped the rag around the tip of the rod, breathed on it, and it suddenly became a glowing flame, giving a clear view of the corridor.

In the distance, there was another timber door; only this one was fitted about twelve feet above the floor, with no means of access up to it.

The young Dreg levitated himself in line with the new door and noticed that it had the same carved animals on it, but they were in a different order.

He removed the key and peered through the Keyhole.

He thought he could see something on the other side, but didn't mention anything to his colleagues.

Once back on the floor, he recalled the order of the animals in each of the door panels on the first door, then he focussed on the new door.

He magically rearranged the animals, the Goat, the Fox, the Dog and the Horse and although they reappeared into the right panels, the Horse started to glow!

'Something is wrong.' Said Alfa. The carved Horse is glowing, I sense we have company, so let's be on our guard!'

The door creaked open very slowly; Alfa asked everyone to join hands again.

They drifted up to the upper door, which Alfa then pushed open. On the other side, they found themselves confronted by a "Ring of Fire"!

The four Dregs were looking within the fiery ring and saw a fearsome Black Stallion, with a figure seated on it. The figure wore black armour, a white cape and he carried a lance.

Alfa shouted to his three colleagues.

'*Quickly*! Called Alfa, find somewhere to cover yourselves; it is Tavet, the evil Horseman, ***and beware, the horse can breathe fire!***'

The evil Horseman raised the horse onto its hind legs, and two shafts of fire were discharged from the steed's nostrils, followed by a booming voice from the evil rider.

'***Dregs, you are trespassing in my space, you are not welcome here, so I must dispose of you all now; you are no match for me!***'

Float and Levi gulped in fear of what they were witnessing.

Alfa asked all three Dregs to follow him along an adjoining corridor as quickly as possible, before Tavet made his move.

Snak called out to Alfa.

'Look, look at the middle of the wall above you, the flames from the Horse must have made the crack, which is starting to grow wider!'

Snak opened his silver box and a shaft of light appeared.

The light found its way into the aperture and appeared to dance around the orifice, until it was inside.

'Quickly everyone, join hands again, *NOW!*' Alfa ordered.

Alfa's orders were greeted with sighs of relief, as they could hear the sound of hooves, getting louder and louder.

The gaping void was now large enough to accept all four dregs, who rapidly floated upwards to it, before passing through, into a damp smelling chamber.

The shaft of light from the silver box was still shining and revealed a stone-built room; a Dungeon!

Once everyone had safely landed, they inspected the area and saw two large gates at the rear of the prison cell.

"Crash, bang", the two large gates started to open on Alfa's command. They only opened slightly, but wide enough to see the ring of fire and the evil Horseman, once again.

Two more shafts of fire, spewed out from the horse.

Tavet spotted the silver box held by Snak and shouted loudly.

'Give me the silver casket dreg and I will allow you all to pass!'

'No, snapped Alfa, leave this place, or prepare to be sent back to hell!'

Alfa reached inside his shirt and pulled out the scroll, two more shafts of fire were emitted from the black horse, just missing Snak!

As the scroll was being unrolled by Alfa, Tavet sensed defeat, as he had been warned of the power it contained.

His eyes were focussed on the silver box and it suddenly disappeared!

Alfa fully unrolled the scroll and shouted out the words contained within. His voice was clear and decisive.

'Spiritus Ex Infernus De'!

The whole area was filled with a swirling wind, dust and smoke, covering the entire dungeon.

The scroll and the silver box, then floated away from the hands of Alfa and Snak's grasp, and were sent into oblivion; then Snak saw that the large steel gates had opened fully, once the swirling wind had died down.

'Quickly everyone, Snak called out, the gates are now fully open!'

The ring of fire had disappeared, Tavet was summoned back, to face the wrath of Malus, due to his failure under Park Lane.

'You have failed me Tavet, where is the Talisman?'
'It disappeared Master, just vanished into thin air. Please forgive me, my lord!' Replied a grovelling Tavet.

'You fool, the dregs had managed to transport it to a safe place; you should have seized it straight away, so now you will pay for your incompetence!'

'You are now banished from here and will be sent to the "Bastille of Pain"!'

Alfa was keen to vacate the Battleground, so that they could find the library. The four Dregs found another staircase, just outside the prison cell, which they descended down to slowly, and once they were at the bottom, they found another timber door, a door with no markings or animals, just a sign above the frame, which read "Library".

The door was unlocked, thankfully, thought Alfa.

They all walked into the very large room, which contained numerous shelves, housing rows of books.

Snak knew where the Almanac was located and pointed out its position to Alfa. Alfa used his powers to remove the Almanac, which then landed onto a large oak table. He opened it up, to reveal the Index pages.

He followed the alphabetic names of each section and stopped on "Lost Objects". He opened the page numbered in the index and began to read the words.

'To locate any object of Literature from Limbo or other unknown places, you must locate the signs of Aries, Libra, then Pisces, and when the three signs are shown together, you will find a Crest!'

All four Dregs were excited over the words contained within the Almanac, but remained quiet.

Alfa then returned the book, back to the same shelf, where he found it.

Levi enquired whether they were any closer to finding the lost Book of Dregs.

'I am not sure at the moment Levi, replied Alfa. I must consult Hermes for further information over the three signs of the Zodiac, before we proceed further.'

They returned to the labyrinth of tunnels and were glad when they'd found their way back to Park Lane.

They proceeded to Snaks home, as he had invited them all to dinner. Snak prepared a lavish feast for his three Dreg friends, after finding various scraps below the Dorchester Hotel.

The meal was devoured with delight by each of the companions and they all agreed that the famous Hotel was certainly living up to its high standards.

Meanwhile, back in the library, the Almanac floated off the shelf it was returned to, earlier that day, then onto the large oak table, once more.

The page stating "Lost Objects" was found.

The book then returned itself to the shelf after the

wording had been read. The invisible force was now on its way to seek the meaning of the three Zodiac signs.

Kalor was now in possession of the information and reassured Malus that he would succeed, after he had found out what the signs being together, meant.

'I will not fail you as Tavet has done Master, I will find out the meaning of the three Zodiac signs and will then put an end to the Dreg civilisation!'

Malus was not convinced.

6: DREGS VERSUS SKELETONS?

Three victorious friends had journeyed to Russell Square the next morning, following the invitation from Hermes, and were greeted with a warm welcome by the wise old Wizard. Snak had agreed not to attend, due to some pressing matters, that needed his attention.

After a debriefing of their previous day's events, Hermes offered the three heroes a grand feast of meat and fruit, together with tea, biscuits and cake, then Dombey and Webley arrived.

'Squeeze in where you can lads, said Hermes and help yourself to some food.'

Hermes passed a plate of meat over to each of the new arrivals and watched as Dombey's eyes grew wider!

Hermes thought about how much there was to discuss and plan, following the clues from the Almanac at the Mount Street library, so he started to scribble things down on a scrap of paper.

'In case I forget,' he mumbled

After discussing their previous day's events, Hermes thanked Levi and Float for their invaluable assistance. Both pals thanked Hermes and Alfa for being asked to help. and offered assist, any time, they were required.

'Don't hesitate to contact us again Prof', sorry, I mean Professor,' said Float.

Back in the room below the British Museum, it was time to decipher the clues, to find out the connection between the Aries, Libra and Pisces signs.

'Alfa, did you retain the key from the upper door below Mount Street?' Asked the old wizard.

'Yes, I did Professor, I didn't need it, but with all the commotion going on, once the door had opened, I forgot to put it back, sorry.'

'No need to apologise my boy. I need to look at the strange designs on it.'

He placed his "Pince-Nez" glasses over his eyes and looked at the designs.

'Here, look at this Alfa, look, there are two fishes on the key, the sign of Pisces! '

Alfa recited from memory, the instructions from the Almanac.

'First look for the signs of Aries, Libra and then Pisces.'

Hermes walked over to his bookshelves and looked for a certain title with a green cover, or was it crimson or black?

The vast rows of books and encyclopaedias were covered with a thick layer of dust.

'Where is that book, he mumbled, where is that book with the green cover?'

'Eureka! he called out, here it is.'

After finding the book, he flicked through each of the pages, then saw the page he was looking for. He laid the book onto the table, then began to recite the words that were detailed on it.

'In the vicinity of Ludgate Hill, in the City of London, there is a building known as the Old Bailey.'

Everyone listened with interest and Dombey grabbed another scrap of food.

'High above the structure there is a statue called "Lady Justice", who holds a sword in her right hand and the scales of justice in her left hand; find this building and you will locate what you seek.'

Dombey and Webley were asked by the old wizard, to assist Alfa with this next part of the quest, but neither of them knew anything about the building, so he searched his memory for someone who lived close to Ludgate Hill.

'You must find my old friend Buck, said Hermes. He will be able to assist you all this time, so please make your way across the city and find Ludgate Hill.'

Alfa returned the key with the two fishes, to his pocket and asked Dombey and Webley to follow him into the tunnels and gulley's, ahead of them.

The three pals then ventured towards Holborn, ready to join the dreg named Buck, and to continue with the next stage of their important quest.

Malus spoke to Kalor, who had managed to find the Almanac at the Park Lane library, which made reference to some signs.

Kalor started to read these details to his master.

'The sign of Libra, and the scales, will be found at a

location known as the Old Bailey, then there is a key with two fishes on the handle, which is the sign of Pisces and lastly, there is the sign of the Ram; Aries.'

Malus confirmed to Kalor that Alfa had the key with the two fishes, which he did not return to its place and warned him that this young Dreg is one to watch closely, due to his unknown strength, and growing powers.

'I am getting tired of these Dregs, Malus roared, we must not fail again, our weakness has been shown to our enemy and hopefully, they will assume that we cannot defeat them. We MUST show them the strong powers we possess; so, do NOT fail me!'

Kalor gave his word to Malus and expressed his determination to destroy the dregs at the Old Bailey; and to find out the meaning of the three zodiac signs.

It was very early, the next morning; the three pals had rested in a tunnel below Fleet Street, which was extremely busy above them.

Above them, there were quite a few vans, small and large, which were transporting that day's newspapers to the newsagent shops, ready for the humans to read and catch up on what was happening in the world.

Alfa did not sleep too well, he thought about the Jinn and why they had failed on two occasions, at Battersea Park, and Park Lane.

He wondered whether they were trying to appear weak, so that the Dregs would make mistakes when they met again.

He knew that there would be more confrontations with the Jinn, that was inevitable he decided.

After waking Dombey and Webley, Alfa produced a few scraps of food for his friends to eat.

Webley consumed another large dose of his medicine and wondered why the bottle was always full.

'Hermes must have replenished it, he thought?

Dombey enquired about the journey that lay ahead for them.

Alfa confirmed that they did not have far to go from where they were, below Fleet Street, but firstly, they would need to locate the station, at Blackfriars, which is where they would find Buck.

The water of the river Thames was very high.

Upon it, there was the usual fleet of pleasure crafts, making their way to various pontoons, to transport the human tourists along the great river, showing them the magnificent, historical sites of London.

Buck lived close to Blackfriars Bridge, which was close to the river Thames, somewhere below the underground and railway stations.

His "shady" looks were emphasised by a brown pin-striped suit, complete with turn-ups, a black shirt and a white tie.

He also wore a brown Fedora hat and a small, unlit cigar in his mouth, giving him the appearance of a gangster.

Alfa had telepathically contacted Buck, confirming that he and two friends would be with him shortly.

The three friends found their way to Blackfriars Bridge.

Dombey looked amazed at the sights before them, he gazed at the vast number of huge "skyscrapers" that looked as though they were touching the white puffy clouds.

'How do we find Buck asked Webley?'

'Hi Mac, called Buck', Webley jumped.

After exchanging greetings, Alfa looked at Buck and wondered whether he could be trusted.

He sensed that the flashy dreg was trouble, due to his manner, but had no choice, as they needed someone to show them the building, with the Lady Justice on its roof.

They drifted through the tunnels and gulley's, then departed a drain close to the Old Bailey, with the Courts of Justice, above them.

Buck pointed at the building's roof, where they saw the figure with the Scales and the sword.

Buck suggested that he should get paid for his services; Alfa responded, and said he would sort something out for him, after they had found the signs of the Zodiac.

He asked each of the dregs to be wary of any danger that could befall them once they were inside, but also, to think hard about what linked the three signs, once they had found them.

Dombey was not amused at the request from Buck. *'I don't trust him,'* he mumbled!

'We must return to the tunnels, shouted Alfa, I sense that we have company again and it's the quickest way to get inside the busy building.'

Buck protested and stated he didn't like the tunnels, resulting in Dombey asking him to "Shut-up", and confirming that he had a job to do.

Buck looked at Dombey and his large frame, then

apologised.

They found their way into some dark winding passages, which were poorly lit, so Alfa produced a long piece of string and tied each of his allies together.

It was very quiet within the winding tunnels, but suddenly, there was a very loud gush of water, which swept all four of them helplessly through the gulley's.

Dombey stretched his strong arms out, hoping that he could grab onto something, but couldn't find any protrusion to grasp.

The gulley's then started to descend, causing the water to flow faster.

Alfa knew he had to do something, then Webley suddenly called out. 'Look, there's a light ahead!' he shouted.

Alfa now realised that they were in an underground reservoir, the City of London's main water supply, as he could hear the sound of machinery.

Water was gushing through the gulley's, which was causing a whirlpool about sixty yards ahead of them.

They had to think fast!

Alfa spotted a large beam ahead of them and concentrated hard!

He undid his pieced of string, then, using levitation, he raised himself out of the water and gripped the beam, then pulled each of his friends out of the stream, to their huge relief.

In all the commotion, Alfa realised he had dropped the Key with the two fishes.

They made their way up to a pathway, just above the beam, and Alfa made sure that everyone was ok.

He spotted a door a little way further along the

pathway and asked his three friends to rest awhile.

Alfa returned to the swirling stream, to look for the key. He fought against the strong current, but it was far too powerful for him.

Dombey saw that his friend was in trouble and tied himself to the steel beam, then jumped down to help his good friend.

Alfa thanked Dombey for saving him, and announced to his allies, that he had lost the key.

Kalor laughed as he held the Key in his evil hand.

'Now, I must find a suitable lock for this Key', he mumbled.

The eerie laughter was very loud and echoed through the tunnels below; each of the Dregs looked ahead, at some long corridors, wondering where the noise was coming from.

They continued along the empty corridors and Alfa had a feeling of "Deja-Vu", when he spotted a large number of panelled doors, similar to the doors he had seen, below Park Lane.

He asked his friends to try each of the doors, to see if any of them were unlocked.

'One of these doors has the sign of the Ram or the scales on it, probably on the other side.' Alfa confirmed. 'So, please check each door very carefully!'.

Every door was closely studied, before attempting to open them, then Webley had spotted a set of scales on three of the panels, of three separate doors; one of which was slightly open!

Alfa felt the presence close by and alerted his friends of the possible danger. He then noticed that Buck had disappeared; he'd gone through one of the doors!

Buck found the door open and had walked through, to check what was behind it. He then spotted the horned Ram, the sign of Aries! Buck wanted to confirm his find, but could not open the door, as it was now locked.

He called for help, but had no response. Nobody could hear his cries, as the large oak door had made the room soundproof.

Buck frantically searched the room and found a faint glimmer of light coming from a gap below another door, directly opposite the one he had come through.

The flashy dreg had managed to open the rear door and spotted someone, or something ahead.

The figure wore green armour and had a blue cape draped over him; he also carried a large sword.

It was Kalor!

The invisible evil force waved the sword in the air and from the sharp tip, came a shaft of light, which surrounded Buck, and placed him into a frozen state.

Kalor had enticed him into the room and laughed at how easy it was to fool the weak dreg.

Alfa became impatient, none of the doors were revealing the sign of Aries.

'Has anyone seen the sign of the Ram, asked Alfa. We need all three Zodiac signs together!'

Alfa sensed the presence of the Jinn again, and quickly summoned the "Sword of Truth".

The blade glowed; the steel shaft became heavier and pointed towards a door, just ahead of him.

Alfa touched the door with the sword, and it passed straight through.

He called Dombey and Webley and asked them to stand behind him, then pushed open the door fully, so that they could all enter the room. He looked around, and asked his two friends to be careful.

'I feel the evil Jinn are present in this room, show yourself, reveal who you are' Alfa called.

He tightly gripped his magic sword for courage; a deep piercing voice was heard, then the green armoured Jinn warrior appeared.

'I am Kalor, you're Master; bow down before me dregs, do as I command, and you will not be harmed!'

Alfa spotted the frozen form of Buck but Kalor raised his sword, then both Dombey and Webley also became frozen where they stood.

Alfa edged towards his three pals and spotted a shape appearing. From within one of the walls, Alfa saw a large wolf.

The valiant dreg waved his magic sword over the wolf, which then exploded into the air.

He tried to release his three frozen friends, but Kalor waved his hands towards the young dreg and tried to freeze him; Alfa was one step ahead, he closed his eyes and suddenly vanished.

The evil warrior also disappeared, but his piercing voice echoed round the chamber, followed by the constant laughing.

'Ha, Ha! Now, we are equal Dreg, now we fight!'

Alfa cringed when he heard the voice and the echoed laughing from Kalor.

Kalor spoke again.

'Now dreg, now you will see what I can do, listen carefully, you will soon understand the meaning of Death!'

Alfa could hear footsteps close by, getting louder and

louder, which sounded like the military marching, he had witnessed at the Chelsea Barracks, soldiers he thought?

He could also hear, what sounded like chains, being dragged along the stone floor.

He couldn't see anything or anyone, so he materialised outside the room and waited, to see what was coming.

This was no ordinary army, this was a Platoon of dead soldiers, summoned by Kalor.

There were twelve, full-size Skeletons, each armed and ready to fight anyone to the death.

Alfa stepped back into the chamber and promptly released each of his friends from their frozen state.

He had noticed earlier, when he was looking for any clues to the Zodiac signs, that there were various weapons and shields, mounted on the upper walls of the room, and he magically armed each of his pals with a suitable weapon, to help him fight the deadly army.

Kalor screeched out in defiance.

'Nobody can defeat the undead, get ready to fight your last battle!'

The dreg army of four, raised their weapons, Alfa with the Sword of Truth, Dombey with an axe and shield, Webley with a smaller sword and shield, and lastly, Buck, who was armed with a spiked club and a shield.

Kalor watched in anticipation, as his skeleton army advanced, but Alfa waved his sword once again; his three dreg friends had now became nine!

The skeletons had now entered the room and began to raise their swords.

Dombey and his three "clones", stood on the front line and swiftly used their huge bodies to barge into the first row of skeletons, causing some of them to fall over, but they quickly arose, unharmed and ready to fight on.

They each thrust their swords into the ribs of the bony soldiers, but the deadly army were unaffected!

Alfa confirmed that he would deal with Kalor and raised his sword to the ceiling; a puff of smoke appeared from the sword's tip.

The smoke encircled a figure, Kalor appeared, again!

Alfa threw the Sword of Truth into the evil figure, and was immediately covered by a blue cape.

Alfa threw the cape aside and tried to retrieve his weapon, but the shaft had become embedded, deeply into the floor.

Kalor materialised, he was foul smelling, with a distorted shape, and surrounded by a green and yellow haze.

Kalor also tried to release Alfa's sword, but he also failed. The evil warrior took refuge behind a large metal cabinet and tried to get his blue cape back, as this was the source of his invisible power, and without it, he was helpless.

The fight continued in the corridor, with the nine dregs boldly and gradually defeating the army of bones, leaving layers of skeletal ribs, arms, legs and skulls, scattered across the floor.

Webley had found a strength he never knew he possessed, Buck fought for his life and Dombey used his sheer weight and weapons, to attack the evil foes.

One of the Dombey clones had managed to loosen one of the heavy doors and promptly pushed it, which landed on two of the bony frames.

He then climbed onto a table and spotted a Battle-Axe

mounted on a wall.

'Alfa, the axe if you please!' Asked the Dombey clone. At once, the heavy axe was released and caught by the clone.

"Thwack", another pile of bones was shattered and spread all over the floor.

The battle at the Old Bailey was in full flow.

Alfa finally managed to release his magical sword, then summoned a bright light to his aid.

Kalor was suddenly blinded by this and dropped the key with the two fishes, which landed magnetically onto the tip of Alfa's blade.

'*AHH!*

Alfa had catapulted the key, which hit Kalor between the eyes, causing him to vanish.

All the remaining skeletons and their weapons disintegrated immediately.

'Hooray,' shouted Webley!

All the dregs and their clones gave out a deafening victory roar.

The dreg clones then disappeared, leaving just the four original friends back in the room; then Alfa magically transported the borrowed weapons back to their original places.

A furious Malus roared his disapproval at the defeated Kalor, who was swiftly banished to the "Bastille of Pain", to join his fellow warrior Tavet!

Back at the room in the courts of Justice, Dombey was staring at a crest above one of the doorways.

'The crest Alfa, look at the crest!' Shouted Dombey.

The three other inquisitive dregs gazed at the crest, but Buck's eyes concentrated on a large treasure chest. They focussed hard at the crest, to see if there were any clues and hadn't noticed that Buck wasn't amongst them.

The crest was mounted on a gold plate and was divided into four sections, with a red crown in its centre.

In the top left-hand section, was an arrow, pointing north. In the top right-hand section, was an identical pair of books.

The bottom left-hand section revealed a huge thin tower and the remaining section also showed two identical books.

Alfa sketched the crest and made sure all the details were there.

Webley picked up the blue cloak that Kalor had left behind, he neatly folded it and passed it over to Alfa.

'We must discuss the detail of the crest with the Professor, said Alfa; he will be able to decipher the items on each of these squares.'

Three dregs made their way out to the corridors where the battle was fought earlier, Buck was nowhere to be seen.

Webley stated that he last saw Buck looking very interested in a large chest, in one of the rooms.

Buck was still there and was trying to lever open the chest with a sword, but failed to notice that the crest his colleagues were looking at earlier, had vanished. He eventually managed to open the trunk and to his amazement, saw it contained numerous jewels, gold coins and other priceless ornaments.

He reached into the Treasure Chest, containing the valuable goods; his greed had got the better of him.

The treasure all started to disappear and Buck was swallowed along with it.

The Jinn now had a Hostage!

Back at Russell Square, Hermes greeted the brave trio and told them that this was becoming a habit and was another victory for them.

'Now, let us check your drawing of the crest please Alfa.', asked Hermes.

Dombey helped himself to some food, the old Wizard had prepared. Webley took another "slurp" from his medicine bottle, and also found something to eat.

Suddenly, there was a vibration coming from the shelves behind Alfa, which caused some bottles to fall off and smash on the ground below.

'Look, green smoke!' shouted Hermes, who swiftly placed his "Pince-Nez" glasses over his eyes and looked into the mass.

A vision appeared within the green haze; it was Buck!

'We wondered where Buck had got to' exclaimed Alfa, we assumed he'd made his way home from the Old Bailey, without saying goodbye?'

Dombey did not like the flashy dreg, but kept it to himself.

The green haze became thicker, Buck disappeared from view and Malus began to speak.

'You can have your greedy friend back, but in return, I want the magical sword and the cloak which belongs to Kalor!'

'*No!* Alfa protested.

'As you wish! I will now give you one of your earth hours to decide, just one hour, no more!'

The old professor advised Alfa that they had no

choice, and had to accept the Jinn's terms.

'Although Buck was captured due to his greed, our laws state that no dreg must be held in captivity, and must be returned back to us, at any cost!'

Hermes explained to his pupils, that the Sword of Truth was powerless to the Jinn and that even greater powers could be summoned, from the Zone of Light.

The sword and the cape, were sent to the dark forces within the time span, much to the annoyance of Alfa.

Buck appeared in the room, as soon as the sword had vanished. Hermes looked over at the dreg, who stood in front of him, with his head bowed in shame.

'A stern lecture is needed here I feel' stated Hermes.

Alfa wondered what other powers were available, as he felt helpless after losing the Sword of Truth.

'Now everyone, called Hermes, we must continue with our search for the clues within the sketch of the crest!'

'So, the thin tower is something we must research, but we also have two sets of books, *hmm*,' Hermes mumbled.

The old wizard confirmed that they would need to enter the library within the museum above his home, to get some idea of the "twin" sets of books.

He advised Dombey and Webley that tomorrow, they would need to search for a different book, once he had remembered the title.

Later, Hermes fell into a deep sleep and his mind concentrated on two things.

Firstly, of how to retrieve the "Sword of Truth"! He could visualise the sword, in the hands of Malus, who would be trying to see what powers it possessed.

'Then the twin books,' he muttered.

Malus addressed another of his evil accomplices.

'Asper, you are the wisest of the Jinn, I trust in your judgement, but the dreg named Alfa is blessed with many powers; powers that seem to be growing stronger, every day!'

'My lord' Asper replied. 'If you trust my judgement, may I please take Belua with me on this mission, with my guidance, we will both be a strong force and together, we will destroy these infidels!'

Malus agreed with Asper's request and referred to the sketch the young Dreg had made of the crest.

He confirmed that they could see the original crest in the Old Bailey, but would wait until the old professor had solved each of the clues.

'Sleep you unworthy Dreg's, Malus whispered, tomorrow, you will solve the clues about the books and we will then make our next move!'

7: THE EYE OF HORUS

Hermes had been awake all night, thinking about how they had to let the Jinn have the "Sword of Truth". He thought about another Talisman to replace it, but he knew the sword had very strong powers, even though, it would be useless to the Jinn. 'Hopefully,' he assumed?

The wise old professor left his humble abode and ventured up to Russell Square above, knowing that it would be too early for the humans to be on their way to work. He saw a large machine with a rotary brush, sweeping up the rubbish from the previous day and thought about the very loud noise it was making.

The sun began to shine through the cotton wool clouds; it was dawn and the start of another day. Some of the golden rays were already concentrating on the roof of the British Museum.

Hermes descended into a nearby drain and found his way through to a gulley below, a tunnel that would take him into the lower depths of the British Museum's library, his most favourite place.

'Now where do I start, and what is it I have come to find here, the absent-minded Wizard muttered. Ah, yes, this is what I have come here for', as he looked at the books, starting with the letter A!

Hermes focussed hard, on endless rows of books. He saw the titles on each of these; Astral Plains, Astrology, but the section he sought wasn't there!

"Ah, Amulets", he cried out!

He spotted three volumes on the subject, which were out of place, but as these were the ones he required, he magically removed them from their shelves and transported them into his study, below the Square.

'It is imperative I find a suitable replacement for the Sword, muttered Hermes; something as powerful as the trusty blade, and something that can assist us in our search for our lost book!'

Hermes made his way back to his study and started to browse through each of the books from the library.

Buck appeared; he'd come to see if the Professor required any assistance.

Hermes knew that Buck wanted to make amends for his behaviour at the Old Bailey, but after all, he was a dreg, and agreed that they could help him.

After reading one of the books, Buck pointed at a page he had found.

The page was creased, and when Buck had smoothed it out, he saw a crest, with a thin tower in one of the squares and two sets of books in another section, both identical to the sketch Alfa had drawn.

Buck, anxious to make up for his deceit, stated that he had seen an inscription on the page and asked if he could read it out. Hermes agreed.

'The "Eye of Horus", Buck read out, what is this eye Professor, what does it mean?'

Hermes felt a weird sensation as Buck read out the inscription and told everyone that this was just what they were looking for, and was a very fortunate coincidence.

He then asked Buck to pass back the book, so that he could study it further.

Alfa, Dombey and Webley, had been woken up by their two excited colleagues and joined them, in the room next door.

The old Professor explained that they had found reference to the thin tower and the two sets of books, purely by coincidence and that the same page had referred to the "Eye of Horus".

He asked everyone to get some breakfast, so that he could check out the clues in the book and advised he would let them all know as soon as possible, as he wanted some "peace and quiet"!

Inside his secret room, Hermes had made some mental notes and soon found what he was searching for, while his colleagues were busy, eating their breakfast.

During their breakfast, the young dregs discussed their excitement over another possible quest, once Hermes had looked at the clues in the book.

The old Professor suddenly called out to his friends and asked them to be quiet, so that he could explain his findings.

He confirmed to his four companions, that the Thin Tower was an Obelisk, which could be found, close to the river Thames, where they would need to search for a ring; a ring that was made out of bone. He also confirmed that he needed to get more information from the book.

'When can we get started Hermes,' Alfa and Dombey called out.

Hermes told them to be patient and wanted to continue with the details, so that they did not miss anything, and, asking them all to remember that the Jinn were becoming even more determined to get their lost book.

After reading the relevant passage from the book, Hermes asked for silence once more, as he wanted to give his pupils some more information over the ring.

'Now all of you, please help yourselves to more food, I need to have a quick word with Alfa, before you all leave.'

Alfa, joined the old professor in his musty smelling secret room, which was full of old Charts and maps of the Solar System. He also saw that Hermes had changed into his Alchemist's robe.

On some of the shelves, Alfa spotted some odd-looking shapes inside glass jars, each of the jars were labelled with its contents. "Powdered Bat Wings", "Foxes Teeth" and "Hair of the Jackal". The young dreg wondered what these were all used for, but did not want to ask.

Hermes laid out several ancient looking scrolls, on a round, badly scratched table, and unrolled each one in turn, to reveal the words contained within them.

He discarded three of the scrolls and explained that the fourth one would reveal some helpful answers over the ring, and of Horus.

He then produced his giant magnifying glass and began to decipher the writings on the fourth scroll, narrating these words to his fellow dreg.

'The legend states that many centuries ago, King Amiz and his Queen, who were rulers of Egypt at that time, were blessed with a wonderful son, who they had named Ra-Bin-Or. He was their only child and would be heir to the throne. The young Prince was given everything he asked for, except freedom, but he yearned for adventure outside the walls of the palace he lived in. Horus, who was a trusted soldier of the King and Queen, was made bodyguard to the boy; his role was to ensure that the young prince was well looked after and kept away from any danger'.

Alfa listened to the story Hermes was narrating, he loved learning about anything to do with history.

'One day, the boy was playing in the Palace Grounds and had managed to evade his bodyguard, by finding a secret passage. The passage led him outside of the Palace walls and into unknown territory, where he quickly searched for things that he had only heard of, but had never seen. The young Prince found his way to the mighty River Nile, just beyond the Palace and decided to paddle in the shallow and inviting water. Horus was summoned, after the queen had found that the prince was missing.'

Everyone was engrossed with this magnificent story, and nobody wanted to miss any of the details.

'Horus was frantically searching everywhere for the young Prince, within the Palace Grounds, when he heard a splash and a scream, outside the walls. The young prince had fallen into the deep water and had been swept away by a strong current.'

'Horus ran to the river and dived into the strong and

fast-flowing waters and although he had managed to grab the boy, the current was far too strong for them both; and their bodies were found several days later.'

Hermes took a deep breath, then continued.

'The King and Queen summoned their wise men and asked them to offer a solution over their sad loss, but nobody could provide a way of bringing Ra-Bin-Or back to life, and preparations were therefore made, for the burial ceremonies.'

Alfa loved this story and wished he could travel to Egypt, one day. Hermes continued to read from the scroll.

'King Amiz and his Queen were distraught; their only child was dead. They arranged for a tomb to be built as a memorial to the young Prince, where both he and Horus would be laid to rest.'

'At the Ceremony, a High Priest called "Bil-Ar", advised the Royal couple that everything was done to try and bring back their only son; Bil-Ar also advised the King that the tomb should be permanently guarded, due to the wealth of treasures that would be placed within. The King agreed and asked Bil-Ar to arrange for the protection, inside, and outside the tomb.'

'Both Ra-Bin-Or and Horus were to be "Mummified" and Bil-Ar was to make sure that the young Pharoah's remains, were protected inside the tomb.'

'One of the finest craftsmen in the land, was summoned to the tomb and was asked to bore a hole into the skull of Horus, just above his eye sockets. They asked him to place a cut diamond into the orifice; which would be known as a "Third Eye"; offering protection, for the late young Prince.'

'The remaining, circular piece of skull was then skilfully carved and made into a ring, which was given to the Queen, as a memory of her late son and Horus.'

Hermes drank some water, before continuing.

'Years later, it is rumoured that Queen Cleopatra had somehow, obtained the ring and named it "The Eye of Horus". Cleopatra travelled the world during her reign and, during a trip to London, had somehow mislaid the ring; but after a detailed search of everywhere she had visited, it was never found.'

Alfa asked Hermes whether there were any clues over the twin books; Hermes asked him to look at his sketch of the crest from the Old Bailey and stated that these were scrolls, not books.

The professor placed his magnifying glass over the scrolls, and saw a small drawing below the words he had just read; it contained an Arrow pointing North and the two scrolls.

He confirmed that the scrolls contained the words as read at the burial ceremony by the High Priest Bil-Ar.

Hermes then continued reading from the book.

'It was also rumoured that the soldiers of Cleopatra had raided the tomb and had removed all the treasures contained inside. Soon after, each soldier had suffered the most horrible death.'

Both Hermes and Alfa shivered at the thought, and knew that Horus was only doing the job he was asked to do.

'The ring, if we can find it, Hermes explained, is our protection from the Jinn and must not be used for anything other than this!'

The old professor and Alfa then returned to their

colleagues, who had been waiting patiently for their next instructions.

'Due to the dangers that we will need to face on this search, the old Wizard stated to his friends; I will join you on this next part of our quest!'

Dombey was excited over the Professor being with them, Webley gulped down some more medicine and asked the Professor for a refill.

Alfa thanked his Mentor, but his thoughts were concentrating on the glass bottles he had seen earlier.

Alfa went back to the secret room and focussed on the bottles. His eyes carefully scanned each one, as he quietly mumbled to himself.

'My instincts tell me that amongst these bottles, there is a very powerful potion, something that will assist us during the mission ahead.'

Alfa removed two of the jars from the shelf, the "teeth of the fox" and the "hair of the Jackal".

Hermes removed other glass jars and confirmed the contents as "powdered bats wings", "Raven's tongue" and "ribs of?

'Ribs of the Centaur!' Alfa exclaimed.

Hermes congratulated the young dreg, knowing that Alfas powers were still growing stronger, each day!

'I need six Rat's teeth and four of the Centaurs ribs please Alfa,' asked Hermes.

These were passed over to Hermes, who then counted them out and placed them onto the table, before placing them into a white handkerchief, which he then placed into his pocket.

The Army of dregs left the abode below the British Museum and made their way through the vast labyrinth of tunnels and gulley's, to start their search for Cleopatra's Needle.

They surfaced just outside the Embankment underground station, opposite the grey murky waters of the river Thames.

The wise old Wizard asked everyone to rest for a while, so that he could catch his breath; he was not as energetic as the younger and enthusiastic dregs were.

He shared out some scraps of food he had bought with him. Dombey's eyes were fixed onto a fruit cake, which was then shared out.

Hermes took out the handkerchief from his pocket and gave it to Alfa to keep safe, explaining that he did not want to lose them.

The river Thames looked very cloudy and the tide was just going out, revealing some areas of sand and a vast number of washed-up articles.

The black Obelisk was ahead of them, the thin tower, which the crest had revealed.

'The ring is somewhere close to the Obelisk, Hermes confirmed. This monument my friends, is called "Cleopatra's Needle"!'

He touched the pillar and could not sense any feelings or vibrations, Alfa also tried, but he too, felt nothing.

Hermes suggested that the Rat's teeth and Centaur ribs should be utilised.

Alfa produced the handkerchief and placed the 10 pieces at the base of the column.

After a few seconds, a dark cloud appeared over the Obelisk, followed by a shaft of red light.

The three Dregs stepped back, leaving Alfa to place his webbed hand into the glowing void.

'There is something inside Professor,' Alfa called out, as the dark cloud and the red shaft of light disappeared. As he removed his hand, his colleagues could clearly see something; it was a white bone ring!

'We now have the Eye of Horus my friends, said Alfa. We have another talisman!'

Alfa was very pleased with himself, as he lifted the ring high, to show his excited pals.

Hermes sensed that the evil forces must be close by and stated that they must all find a safe place to calm down, before planning their next move.

'Let's go to my home everyone', suggested Alfa. Everyone agreed.

They returned to the tunnels below the Embankment underground station, then onwards below Green Park, then St James Park, and finally, to The Mall.

Although the home was very small, Alfa made his friends very welcome, and they all commented on the amount of Royal memorabilia neatly placed on his shelves.

He rustled up some food and drinks to consume and asked Hermes if he would check out the ring.

The large magnifying glass appeared from nowhere, which Hermes placed over his right eye.

Alfa passed him the white ring; Hermes studied it carefully and spotted an inscription around the inside.

'Alfa, do you still have the handkerchief I gave you earlier' asked Hermes.

A puzzled looking Alfa reached into his pocket and pulled out the white ragged cloth and passed it to the Professor, who placed the ring inside and turned the ring into a walking stick.

'Oh, dear exclaimed Hermes, I seem to have turned the ring into a cane, now how did that happen?'

Hermes then dropped something into Alfa's pocket and asked to him to keep the handkerchief safe. (Alfa looked even more puzzled)

They returned to join the other friends, at the other end of the small room, who were still eating and drinking.

Hermes gave the Cane to Dombey, and asked the large dreg to keep it safe. Dombey also looked puzzled, but was glad he was able to help.

Alfa knew that the wise old Wizard was up to something.

Malus watched the events with interest, from his dark castle, paying particular interest to the cane, that had been passed over to the large dreg called Dombey.

'So, they think they can fool me, (laughing loudly) but I can wait and watch what they do next, then when the opportunity arises, I will steal the cane!'

Above the home of Alfa, the Mall was quite dark and very busy with the traffic, transporting the humans back to their homes or to another venue, after they had finished their work.

Everyone was invited to stay overnight at The Mall, so that they could plan their next move and make an early start, the next day.

Dombey peered out of a small orifice, spotting the bright full moon above and pointed the cane at it, when all of a sudden, a bright green flash appeared.

The cane immediately vanished.

Webley and Buck looked at a very surprised Dombey, then over to Hermes and Alfa, who were laughing.

Dombey started to offer his apologies for what had occurred, but the wise old dreg, explained that the cane was in fact a handkerchief, not the ring and that he had to check whether they were being watched.

Alfa produced a various assortment of fruit for his friends and asked his colleagues to "tuck-in", but Webley was still puzzled over what was going on, so he swiftly guzzled a dose of his red medicine.

Hermes quietly thought to himself that this was the work of the Jinn and that they would be raging, once they had found they had been duped.

Malus was left holding a piece of cloth when he had started to inspect the cane. His two evil aides, Asper and Belua, knew that even their Master was capable of failure, but did not dare to mention this, to the irate evil leader.

Malus knew he had failed and told his aides that they must be patient and not to be drawn into a confrontation at this time, but confirmed that the dregs had found something of value in the Obelisk; something that he wanted, and patience was required until their foe had made their next move.

Hermes asked Alfa if he still had the sketch of the crest, as he felt that something was missing.

Alfa passed the sketch over to his master.

'When you drew this sketch my boy, what did you rest the paper on?'

Alfa explained that he had rested the paper onto an old

book that was lying on a table.

'That explains why there is a faint word on your sketch,' mumbled Hermes.

The old wizard ran a piece of charcoal over the letters.

'The word, from what I can make out is spelt T-Y-B-U-R-N and this is becoming very confusing?'

Hermes spoke of a place called Tyburn, from many years ago, telling his friends that it was a place of Execution, where criminals were hanged.

Alfa asked if this had anything to do with Tyburn Way, close to Marble Arch and close to Park Lane.

'YES, my boy, yes that is it, the Hanging Tree in Tyburn Way is the next place we must seek, so tomorrow we are going to the Gallows!'

Hermes was happy that they had found another clue and wanted to speak to all his pupils, but there was a deathly silence in the room, as they had already heard what was said.

He suggested that they all got a good night's sleep, as there was a very important day ahead of them. The old professor checked on everyone a little while later, before retiring to his bed.

The forces of evil were planning their next move.

'Tyburn, that's all I could hear Master!' Stated Belua.

'You have done well Belua, said Malus; we will search for this place, if we have to, but the Dregs will probably lead us to it first!

8: IN THE SHADOW OF THE GALLOWS.

Alfa awoke early the next morning, he had asked Hermes not to wake Dombey, Webley, or Buck and that he would make contact with them, should they be required.

Hermes had also woken early and had been reading a book on the place called Tyburn.

He spoke to Alfa before he was about to leave, confirming that he had transported the book from his home in Russell Square.

'I used something called Telekinesis, another power that you will learn about, one day, my boy.'

Alfa couldn't wait, he was happy to learn new powers!

'The book gave me an idea of what Tyburn was all about;' and proceeded to give Alfa a brief description.

'Many years ago, society in London was corrupt, as there was hardly any work, resulting in crimes being committed; crimes that got steadily worse over the years. The humans were sent to prison for the crimes they had committed and, in some cases, were tried for murder. If they were found guilty, they were sent to the Gallows!'

Alfa gulped, and shivered, when he heard the word "Gallows", again

'The High Courts of Justice in those days, passed the sentences down through a notorious Magistrate named Judge Jeffries, also known as the "Hanging Judge"!'

Alfa loved listening to historic stories, even if they were gory subjects.

'This judge condemned the guilty persons and sent them to the Gallows, to the place called Tyburn!'

The book suddenly disappeared and was returned safely to the old professor's home, below the British Museum.

Alfa shivered again, at the thought, but was consoled by his Master, stating that the infamous tree had now gone, and that Tyburn Way, near Marble Arch was so named, to mark the exact location of the tree.

Alfa said farewell to Hermes, and made his way alone to Marble Arch, using the tunnels and gulley's below. On his way there, he had contacted Snak by telepathy, asking him to join him at Speaker's Corner.

Snak was already there, as he lived below the Dorchester Hotel not too far away, and wondered why his friend had asked him to meet him there.

Snak had a bundle around his shoulders, which contained some food he had salvaged earlier from the Dorchester Hotel. He had just pulled out a large chicken leg and was about to take a bite from the tasty looking morsel, when Alfa called out to him.

The two friends greeted each other and discussed a brief outline of their mission.

Alfa also mentioned to Snak, about how Hermes had managed to trick the Jinn, into thinking that the talisman had been changed into a walking stick, which was actually, a handkerchief.

Snak nearly choked on the chicken leg when he heard the tale.

The two friends started to make their short journey, through the tunnels from Speakers Corner, and soon landed below Tyburn Way, close to Marble Arch, ready for their continuing quest.

During their journey, Alfa also explained to Snak about what took place at Tyburn all those years ago, but specifically stated that the Gallows were no longer there.

'From now on, we must be cautious, stated Alfa, as the Jinn may be close by, and were probably watching our every move.'

Snak remembered his encounter with the Jinn, when they were not too far from here, in Park Lane.

'They have been duped over the talisman, said Alfa, so they will be even more ruthless in their aim, when they see the new talisman!'

The two allies found Tyburn Way, not knowing where to start looking, or what they were looking for. All they could see were the human tourists aimlessly looking for any clues about the infamous "Hanging Tree".

Alfa produced the ring and showed it to Snak, who asked what powers the piece of bone had, but Alfa did not reply.

'Here is the area my friend, said Alfa; this is where the old tree was located, so now, we must stay close together and be aware that we may be being watched!'

Malus was watching the two dregs through a hazy mist. He summoned Asper and Belua to his side; the two evil servants hastily joined their master.

Malus pointed out the spot where the two dregs were, and asked them both to listen carefully to him.

'Asper, although you managed to succeed in capturing one of the dregs, you must still be wary of their powers, but do not be fooled, these dregs always seem to have something powerful in their possession and they somehow managed conceal something they had found from the Obelisk.'

'Whatever it is, you must bring it to me!' He roared.

'Belua, you will accompany Asper, so go, both of you and remember, we need to be one step ahead of them this time; do not reveal yourselves until you have located the talisman, which is called "The Eye of Horus", I want this amulet, so do **not** fail me!'

Snak was still eating the scraps of food from his bundle; Alfa had thanked him for wanting to share, but stated that he wasn't hungry.

Snak was busy wiping his greasy webbed hands and noticed a large circle of grass ahead of them, which he pointed out to his friend.

'Good work Snak, I think you have found what we seek!'

They both moved closer, to check the grass patch and Alfa, based on his intuition, agreed that it was the exact spot, where the Hanging Tree once stood.

Alfa passed the ring over to Snak and asked him to keep it safe and not to let it out of his sight.

They both disappeared; Alfa asked Snak to stay silent,

as he pointed to the crowd of humans ahead.

The two dregs had gone back in time, the hanging tree was ahead of them, and several humans were about to be executed, witnessed by a large crowd of sightseers!

The military and a surgeon were on guard, to ensure that the unfortunate persons were hanged by the neck until they were deceased, based on the sentences passed from the court and the infamous "Hanging Judge".

Snak ran towards a nearby bush, so that he could not be seen, or have a view of the executions, but Alfa confirmed that they were both invisible; so Snak checked to make sure he still had the ring in his pocket.

The two evil forces were now standing over the grass circle on Tyburn Way, which had a blue mist over the spot where the two dregs had disappeared from.

They spotted the scraps of food within the circle and knew that the dregs had recently been there.

Asper asked Belua to wait for his command.

'We must be careful and not be seen, Asper called out. I will become invisible, but you must change your appearance!'

Belua changed himself into a large black cat, then both the Jinn warriors leapt into the blue mist.

Snak spotted a human ahead of him and called to Alfa, asking him to look at the person who was writing something.

They both climbed a small tree close to the human, so that they could get a better look, to see what had been written.

"Let it be recorded, that on this day, four robbers, two Highwaymen and a murderer, are to hanged by their necks until proof was agreed that they had died".

The writer then called out to a human standing next to him and asked him to read, sign and seal the letter.

After reading the text, a stick of red wax was produced, then a flame was applied under the stick, causing drops of the wax to rest on the paper.

The paper was then signed as witnessed, by a quill pen, followed by the King's seal being stamped, over the warm wax.

Alfa wanted to get closer to the document, but sensed something strange about the wooden seal.

Snak waited in the tree as instructed by his companion.

Alfa stared at the design on the seal, it was a large crest on what looked like an orb or a ball, together with a cross, then stored the details into his memory.

Just then, he heard a cry from the tree where Snak was hiding, he had fallen out!

'I was pushed Alfa, there was somebody or something in the tree.' Snak confirmed.

Alfa looked at the tree and saw a large black cat, he knew that the Jinn were close by and asked Snak for the ring.

Just then, in the shadow of the gallows, they were both startled by the sudden silence from the crowd, followed by a loud cheer

Then they saw a man's body dangling at the end of a rope. They both started to look for a hiding place and were followed by the black cat.

A large flash of lightning struck the ground in front of the fleeing pair.

'Stop Dregs, called Asper, you cannot escape from me, now give me the ring!'

The young apprentice calmed down his ally and told him that he would deal with the Jinn warrior.

Snak reached into his pocket and removed the ring, following the request from Alfa.

Alfa held up the ring in defiance, then willed the talisman to disappear.

Asper gave out a loud echoing laugh and confirmed that he was now in possession of "The Eye of Horus"!

Alfa wrongly assumed that the ring had been sent to limbo, but now, it was in the hands of the Jinn.

'This new evil warrior has stronger powers,' thought Alfa, then realised it was Asper, based on the descriptions from Hermes.

Belua appeared back to his own form and was sent back to the present day by Asper, with the ring he would take back to Malus.

Asper briefly remained, thinking about the clue the two dregs had spotted on the paper, which revealed a ball and cross. The blue mist then disappeared; Alfa and Snak were stranded in time and the ring had gone.

Alfa summoned all the powers he had, trying to get the two of them back to the present day, but to no avail.

He wondered whether the ring was the only way to get back, but it was now held by the Jinn.

The two tired dregs searched for a quiet place, away from the noisy melee and the evil warriors.

They had to find somewhere safe, so that they could think of a way to get back home.

Asper had returned and spoke to Malus, confirming that the dregs were stranded at Tyburn and that he had heard about a crest, with a ball and cross, that was carved onto a wooden seal.

Malus congratulated Asper for his victory and confirmed that they now had the Eye of Horus, as bought back by Belua.

'Asper, my victorious warrior, said Malus, you must now go to Kensington to seek the place called the Victoria and Albert Museum. Here you will search for a book, which will show many pictures of Churches and Cathedrals; a book that you will bring to me. I will check the powers of the ring while you are on your mission!'

Malus confirmed that he had released Tavet from the "Bastille of Pain" and that he would join Asper at the Museum.

Alfa and Snak had slept overnight in their hiding place and looked across to the Gallows, which looked even more eerie, due to the missing crowds.

All that was left were the lengths of rope, the decaying bodies and the scavenging birds, eating the flesh.

Alfa had spoken to Hermes by telepathy, who had confirmed how they could return to the present day.

Alfa called Snak and asked him to join hands, then to think and repeat the events of the previous day, the things they could remember, but in reverse order.

The two of them held their hands together, then repeated, "The Black Cat, The Hanging Tree, The Soldiers, the Mist, the Food, then closed their eyes ,and safely returned to Tyburn way, in the present day!

Alfa thanked Snak for his help and asked him to return to the Dorchester Hotel, and that he hoped to see him again, soon, as there would be more missions soon.

Snak said he was happy to help and that he looked

forward to joining the young warrior again, whenever he could be of assistance.

Hermes consoled Alfa, after joining the old professor, at his home in Russell Square.

He told Alfa that they could not beat the Jinn every time and also, that the ring would be on no use to the evil forces.

They spoke about the Ball and the Cross, Alfa had seen on the seal, at Tyburn.

Hermes knew of a book, a book with the title "Churches and Cathedrals of Britain".

He sat down to relax, then searched his memory, trying to remember where he had seen it, and recalled seeing some very high bookshelves, with thousands of books.

Hermes started to drift off to sleep, followed by loud snoring from his gills.

'Ball and Cross, Churches, Cathedrals, he mumbled, where I have seen these before?'

Alfa was used to the old Wizard dozing off and mumbling, but the snoring was extremely loud!

'Museum, Museum of Arts, Victoria and Albert,' Hermes muttered in his sleep.

Alfa knew of the Museum, but was distracted by smoke and flames. Hermes had probably been cooking his lunch earlier, he thought.

He saw through the flames that had changed colour and could make out rows and rows of books, all lined up on very high shelving, with long ladders to access them.

He could also make out the shape of a figure on a horse, surrounded by a ring of fire, it was Tavet, the Evil Horseman; his old foe under Park Lane and now, somehow, the Jinn had beaten them, to their next clue.

Hermes suddenly awoke and confirmed that Alfa should go to the Victoria and Albert Museum in Kensington and find the high bookshelves, where he would find the book of Churches and Cathedrals.

Alfa confirmed that the Jinn were already there, they had obviously seen the Ball and Cross on the wooden seal, but there was no time to question how, it was time to go to the Museum.

'Calm down my boy, we know that the evil Horseman is already there, but who is with him?' (Hermes had also seen the images in the fire)

'It must be Asper, Alfa cried, he would have been at Tyburn and had probably been watching us closely, so he must have seen the wooden seal!'

The old Wizard asked his young apprentice to stay calm, so that he could think about the book again.

He then pointed to a glass jar on one of his shelves and asked Alfa to remove it. Alfa wondered whether it was the right time to be making a potion, but when he picked up the jar, it was full of ashes.

Hermes explained that it was an old friend of his, someone who had looked into Aspers eyes.

He wanted to remind his young apprentice of the dangers ahead.

Tavet had found the book on Churches and Cathedrals and confirmed this to Asper, asking him to search through each page, to see if there was any reference to a Ball and Cross.

Each page revealed the location of Churches, Temples, Chapels and other places of worship. (Both of the Jinn warriors looked at every page with revulsion)

Asper grew impatient, as they could not find any reference to a Ball and Cross.

All he could see, were external drawings of each building, but with no internal details.

'We must have the wrong book Tavet, roared Asper. Search again, and find the correct book, NOW!'

After thinking again about the book, Hermes confirmed to Alfa, that certain books from the Victoria and Albert Museum were often sent to other Museums or similar venues and that he was sure the library in the British Museum above them, may hold the book they required. Alfa was relieved, he did not want to meet the evil Asper, or Tavet again.

Both Asper and Tavet were in a heated argument over where the book was located.

Malus had been watching his two evil warriors and told them that they did have the right book, but to look more closely, as they must have missed something.

After another search of the book, Tavet confirmed that he had found something; it was a Church with a large domed roof and on the top of the roof, was a large ball and cross.

Malus recognised the building and ordered the two warriors to make their way to Ludgate Hill, where they would find the building with the next clue.

'Go to St Paul's Cathedral,' Malus confirmed; search this place, before the dregs find out the correct location!'

Hermes had found a duplicate of the Churches and

Cathedrals book, and had found a page showing St Pauls Cathedral, with a large domed roof above it.

The Ball and Cross they had been looking for, was perched high above the famous cathedral, which was located on Ludgate Hill, in London.

They returned to the old Professors rooms below the museum, and discussed their next move, not knowing whether the Jinn had already found the building, on Ludgate Hill.

Alfa was still thinking of his episode at Tyburn, and did not want to experience failure, again.

Hermes explained that he would need to concentrate on getting the next clue at St Pauls and if the Jinn were already there, then they would need to be careful.

'The aim was still to get back the Book of Dregs, stated the old wizard, and it could only be found by solving the clues but unfortunately, we will always be faced with possible dangers, along the way!'

Alfa slept soundly and was dreaming about getting back the Book of Dreg Civilisation.

He also thought of his next quest at the Cathedral and wanted to make sure he would be ready to face anything the Jinn disciples would throw at him, when they would next encounter them!

'Who shall I contact this time, who will be strong enough to assist me?' He muttered to himself?

9: A CLASH IN THE WHISPERING GALLERY.

Ludgate Hill was extremely busy; there were Buses and Taxis dropping off the hordes of workers and amongst them, were the early morning tourists, who would have to wait a long time, before the cathedral would be open to the public.

St Pauls Cathedral stood 344 feet above the ground, with its outstanding Architecture and majestical features, catching its focus, from most of the crowds passing by.

The sun was shining over the Historic building, which emphasised the large Ball and Cross on its massive roof; then some dark clouds started to drift over, and settled directly above it.

Dombey and Webley were making their way to the venue, after Hermes had contacted them. He had warned them once again, about the dangers they may encounter.

He had also told them, that somehow, the Jinn were beginning to be one jump ahead of them and were becoming even more cunning!

Alfa greeted his two close friends once more and suggested they quickly descend to the tunnels below, as drops of rain were starting to fall.

All three of them had found their way into the nearest drain, just before heavy Thunder and Lightning started.

The thunder was very loud and bolts of lightning seemed to be concentrating, in the vicinity of the magnificent Cathedral.

The three companions had surfaced inside the Churchyard, trying to keep close and to avoid any human sightseers in the area.

Webley swallowed a dose of his medicine and suddenly realised he was on his own, as his friends had disappeared.

Webley started to panic and called out to his colleagues, but there was no response.

Alfa knew that time was important and assured Dombey that they would need to carry on without Webley, for now, and that they would look for him as soon as possible.

The two remaining dregs had found their way to a very cold chamber, which poorly lit, and had a very musty smell.

Dombey started to shiver and was informed by Alfa, that they were in the Crypt. The pair then saw a shaft of light, and started to walk towards it, but it seemed to get further away, after each step.

Alfa produced a map of the Cathedral, which Hermes had given to him, but the poor lighting made it difficult to read and get an idea of where to go next.

They finally reached a doorway, where the light had been shining through and found a set of winding stairs directly outside.

Alfa checked the map and confirmed to Dombey, that the stairs were the access to the "Whispering Gallery".

'Don't worry Dombey, there are only all six hundred and twenty-seven steps to the top, said a smiling Alfa!

Dombey looked decidedly uneasy about climbing so many stairs and started to feel hungry; again!

Webley had somehow found his way to the stairway before his two friends had, and started to climb; but he kept looking, in case he was able to hear, or see his pals.

He called out several times, but the building was empty, causing his voice to echo everywhere. He had managed to climb over three hundred steps, but they seemed to go on, forever.

He knew he was eventually going to be in the Whispering Gallery, and his instincts told him that he should climb to the top of the endless staircase.

Both Alfa and Dombey were not far behind their lost pal, but didn't realise the echo's they had heard, were actually, coming from Webley.

Dombey was reassured by his mentor, that Webley was in no danger and that they would eventually meet up, as Alfa had been using his growing powers, to guide the lost dreg to the correct place.

Webley had found the final stairs and was now in the "Whispering Gallery". He looked around, for a safe place to rest, due to climbing all 627 steps, and sat down, placing his medicine bottle by a huge pillar, then gazed up at the large dome above.

The remaining pair had climbed over four hundred steps and could see the large dome above them.

Alfa could sense something was wrong, he felt that an

eerie presence was close by, and knew the Jinn were inside the Cathedral; he then asked Dombey to be very careful, as they had company!

Webley suddenly looked up, and saw a black horse, surrounded by a ring of fire, with flames spouting from its nostrils. It was the evil Horseman, Tavet!

He knew he was in danger, but his past experiences with the Jinn told him he must defend himself.

Webley looked at his medicine bottle and picked it up; then, with all the strength he could muster, threw it at the evil Jinn warrior.

Tavet had seen the glass bottle coming towards him and raised his sword for protection. The bottle could not penetrate the ring of fire and smashed into a pillar, resulting in many glass shards, appearing and the mixture spilling out and making a large puddle on the surface.

Alfa and Dombey had a further twenty steps left to climb and could just about see the clash, between their friend and the evil horseman in progress.

They had also heard the fragments of the bottle, which had shattered, ahead of them.

Sensing that help was coming for the lonely dreg, Tavet waved his sword, causing Webley to vanish.

The two dreg pals had finally scaled the remaining steps and could only see the remains of the shattered bottle, the puddle of medicine and a scorched area on a pillar close by.

'Tavet was here, Alfa cried out. It looks like he has taken Webley as a hostage!'

In anger, Dombey called for the evil force horseman to show himself.

Immediately, two burning shafts of flames were snorted from the nostrils of a large black horse.

Alfa just managed to push Dombey out of the way and looked around, to see where the evil horseman was.

Whoooooosh! Two more shafts were emitted, scorching the tiled floor, and the pillar, once more.

From within a nearby Marble statue, these events were being monitored by Asper. The invisible Jinn warrior was waiting for the right moment to unleash his evil powers.

Webley was suspended in limbo, he could see everything, but could do nothing.

Alfa had leapt onto the edge of a balcony, in order to avoid the flames, from Tevet's black horse, but another burst quickly followed and was aimed directly, at the young dreg.

Alfa lost his balance and slipped away from the balcony, causing the evil horseman to pull his chargers reigns and rear in triumph.

Alfa had managed to grab a protruding gargoyle below the railings and held on tightly; he didn't want to look below him, as he knew he was very high up.

Tevet roared with laughter, and addressed the clinging dreg below.

'So, you think you can beat me again little beast, your sorcery is useless and will not help you now!'

Alfa realised his predicament and wondered why he always had to rely on his magic, knowing that he was quite agile and could use his own strength.

Tevet and his mount started to move in closer to the clinging dreg; his black horse was ready to snort more flames from his flared nostrils.

Dombey had appeared from behind the pillar and started shouting at the evil horseman, allowing Alfa time to pull a piece of string from his pocket, then, with his spare hand, looped the string and pulled it tightly around the Gargoyle.

Tavet could see Alfa struggling and began to move closer to the balconies edge.

Alfa had tied the piece of string around his waist and had slowly started to winch himself back up to the landing. He then remembered the "Telekinesis" Hermes had shown him, so he focussed on the shattered glass fragments and the puddle of medicine, which suddenly started to form a familiar shape.

A silhouette emerged from the mass.

'You cannot harm me with your feeble magic dreg!' Tavet sensed Alfa was thinking of retaliation.

The fragments of glass and the red mixture formed together and transformed into Hermes, who brushed himself down. He knew his friends were having a difficult time at the Gallery and Alfa had used his powers, to alert the old professor.

Tavet saw who it was and took his evil eyes away from Alfa. The young dreg was then able to climb back over the balcony.

Tavet was ready for him!

Dombey had to think fast, he threw his arms into the air and screamed at the evil horseman. The horse reared and Tavet roared, once more.

'So, we have another dreg here and a very chubby one!'

Dombey hated being referred to as being "chubby", as he always stated it was muscle!

Alfa thanked his friend for the distraction, but the Black Stallion had reared once again and its front legs were hovering over Dombey.

The black horse emitted two shafts of flames from its nostrils, which then formed into a ring of fire.

Dombey could feel the heat.

Asper knew it was now time to make his move and began to emerge from within the marble statue.

Dombey felt a strange tingle all over his body.

Alfa telepathically told him to drop to the floor, then to roll away from Tavet and his stallion.

He also asked him to cover his eyes, as Asper had appeared, who was protected by a force field.

Hermes picked up an object from the floor, which he placed into one of his pockets; and ran over to Asper.

'So, we have the old Wizard joining us well, today!' Yelled Asper.

Hermes carefully tipped his professor's hat over his eyes, to make sure he did not look into the deadly stare, from the evil Asper.

Alfa stood between Dombey and Tavet, desperately trying to think of how he could defeat the evil horseman, while Hermes was busy with Asper.

At that moment, a terrible stench had filled the atmosphere, a cloud of green smoke and a ring of fire, had surrounded a huge figure.

The figure emerged from inside the mist and ring of fire, and its loud footsteps were heard!

Everyone looked around, but could not see where the footsteps were coming from.

Tavet looked over his shoulder, and Asper hovered over the area, shielded by his protective force field.

A large mummified corpse had appeared through the green mist; it was Horus!

Hermes had managed to decipher the inscription on the bone ring, when he had it, which allowed the mummy to appear. The words, when spoken correctly, would summon the mummy, from the dead.

The stench was overpowering, a body from thousands of years ago was once again, walking the earth.

Dombey hid behind the Marble statue where Asper had come from; Hermes called on Asper to face him without the force field.

Horus walked slowly towards the black stallion, Tavet pulled the reins of his horse and now faced the oncoming mummy.

Horus raised both his arms when the horse drew closer, which made the black stallion suddenly bolt, throwing his master to the ground.

Hermes was now facing Asper, but not looking at his eyes. The evil Jinn warrior had been waiting a long time to confront the old Wizard and the time had now come.

'Now, old Wizard, face me, look into my eyes!' Roared Asper.

Hermes felt as though he was being hypnotised, but managed to reach into his deep pocket and produce the object he had picked up earlier. He then suggested to Asper, that he should look at himself.

Alfa had transformed some of the smashed medicine bottle fragments, into a mirror, which Hermes placed in front of Asper.

The evil foe tried to find somewhere to hide, but it was too late; he was looking at his own face, within the mirror, making him disappear!

Tavet ran to retrieve his horse. His screams were echoing loudly across the magnificent Cathedral, as he tried to catch his "spooked" steed.

The black stallion was now running down the corridor, with his evil master behind it.

Horus walked towards the ring of fire and smoke and started to disappear.

'Thank you, my lord Horus, said the old wizard. We may need your services again!'

Webley reappeared and called out to the old professor, but Hermes was already one step ahead and produced a new bottle of the red medicine for his friend.

The four dregs laughed loudly, which echoed throughout the entire, internal areas, of St Pauls Cathedral.

Hermes made sure everyone had recovered from their ordeals and confirmed that they still had a job to do!

The Whispering Gallery contained many statues, paintings and crests, so each of the dregs were asked by Hermes, to search carefully for something of significance.

'We need something to help us find the next clue, something that is related to our quest.' Confirmed the old wizard.

Malus was seething. His two failed warriors stood before him, with their heads bowed down.

'Again Tavet, you have failed me! Be gone from here, I will deal with you later!'

Asper felt dejected, he was not used to defeat and he now faced his master's wrath, and expected to be punished for his failure.

'You, Asper, roared the Prince of Curses, you are a disgrace to the Jinn, and being beaten by an old Sorcerer is unacceptable!'

'But!' Asper tried to plea for mercy.

'Silence! Now, because of you and that bungling Horseman, we are no closer to finding that accursed "Book of dregs"!'

Asper started to fear what would happen, but was relieved, when Malus shouted at him, once again!

'Go now, before I really lose my temper!'

The dregs were still searching for clues at the Gallery. Alfa used his powers to assist in the search, but could not find anything relating to their quest.

Webley was still shaking over his disappearance earlier, and sat down beside one of the many statues. He then opened up his new medicine bottle for a dose, but spilt a few drops onto a plaque at the base of a sculpture.

Hermes spotted the spillage and produced a handkerchief from his pocket, then wiped away the droplets. He noted with interest, the words stated on it, which he read out.

'Where the Stars of the Sky meet the Images of Man. Well done, Webley!' Shouted Hermes.

Alfa and Dombey ran over to look at the plaque; the old professor asked them to look at the words that were inscribed on it.

Webley was still wondering why he had been congratulated?

Hermes suggested that they now leave St Pauls Cathedral and return to Russell Square, where he could decipher the words. Before leaving the gallery, he magically made all the stains, the scorching and other marks, to disappear.

The Whispering Gallery was now silent and showed no signs of the earlier clash, between the Dregs and the Jinn.

The four dregs ascended from the tunnels below and up to the familiar home of Hermes, in Russell Square, unaware that Malus was watching them, again.

'Every time I send my Warriors to deal with these dregs, they are defeated, thought Malus. I feel it is now time to reveal myself to these annoying infidels, and must come up with a way to defeat them!'

He remembered that he had confronted them once before, on the Tree Walk at Battersea Park, but his physical appearance was hidden that time!

Hermes made sure that everyone had eaten some food he had provided, washed down with plenty of Ginger Beer.

When he saw they were all comfortable, he went off to his secret room and gathered some charts, which he unrolled and laid out, over the table.

He had written down the words from the plaque, earlier and recited them quietly to himself, to stop anyone overhearing them.

'Where the Stars of the Sky meet the Images of Man, here you shall find the sign of the lost!'

He searched his charts and could not find anything relating to the Stars and Images of Man. He went to his favourite bookshelves and removed an old dusty book.

He sat down on his comfortable chair and placed his

pince-nez over his eyes, so that he could read the large book, which was an Encyclopaedia.

He started mumbling to himself, while he was reading one of the many pages, from the large encyclopaedia.

'Hmm, Stars, Images of man, duplications, Waxworks!'

'Waxworks, Images of Man, where the Stars meet, yes, I have found it!'

Both Dombey and Webley looked at the professor, as he walked into the room carrying a large Encyclopaedia and looking very pleased with himself.

He explained that on the Marylebone Road, in London, close to Baker Street, there were two buildings close to each other.

Alfa had heard of these places before, but continued to listen, to the old wizard.

'The Planetarium and Madame Tussauds, continued Hermes; where the Stars, meet the images of Man. These are the places we seek!'

He further explained to the perplexed pair that the Planetarium displayed the Planets and the stars, and that the Waxwork Museum, called Madame Tussauds, housed the mages of man, waxwork dummies!

'If you say so professor, said Dombey?'

Hermes suggested to Dombey and Webley that they should ease up on the Ginger Beer.

Hermes called Alfa into his secret room, and asked if he felt strong enough to search for the next clues.

Alfa agreed and asked if he was to take Dombey and Webley to assist him, again.

'Not this time my friend, they are both about to fall asleep in the dining room, probably due to the exhausting episode with the Jinn earlier, but I do have someone else in mind!'

Hermes remembered he had an uncle, close by!

'I feel that my cousin Slooth will be able to help you this time, stated the wise old sage.'

He confirmed to Alfa, that he would make contact with his cousin, who would benefit the next quest and give the other's time to rest awhile.

He told Alfa that he was to make his way to Baker Street, where he would meet with Slooth, who resided in the depths below 212b, Baker Street, near Marylebone Road, which was quite close, to the next two venues.

Alfa thanked the professor for his hospitality, and confirmed he would make his way over to Baker Street the next day, so that he could get some rest, before continuing with the quest.

Hermes telepathically contacted his cousin Slooth and confirmed that Alfa would be with him, somewhere near his home in Baker Street, tomorrow.

He also told Slooth about both the Planetarium and the Waxworks, where they would need to search for some clues, to help them find their lost book.

Slooth knew these places very well, he often visited these venues and looked forward to seeing Alfa for the mission. Alfa found his way into the tunnels and gulley's, below Russell Square and eventually found a place to rest for the night, somewhere below Harley Street, on the corner of Marylebone Road.

10: ELEMENTARY MY DEAR ALFA!

It was overcast in Harley Street, West London, and, if you stared at the grey clouds, you could imagine they were faces, or even animals.

There were rows of Victorian terraced houses, lining both sides of the street, which were either residential, or small businesses.

A number of the houses had a brass plaque fitted outside, stating that they were Doctors, or there were blue ones, confirming the dates, that somebody famous had once lived there, for that period.

The only evidence of the present day, was the noisy automobiles, and not the Horses and Carriages, from the old days.

Alfa woke up quite early after resting below Harley Street, he was thinking about Slooth, the cousin of Hermes, whom he would be meeting that day, somewhere in Baker Street.

He wondered what Slooth would look like, and whether he had the same looks and mannerisms as his cousin; the old professor.

Slooth was busy tidying his small abode, which was full of books, either stacked untidily on shelves, or just lying on the floor.

The books were mainly old volumes relating to Criminology, or anything to do with the Justice system, mainly in the UK, or in other places, across the world.

He also had large stacks of paperwork scattered around, which contained notes of many offences that had been committed. Slooth spent most of his time investigating crimes, involving unlawful acts, that had been carried out, and would research every case, to prove whether the person was guilty, or innocent.

He had a tweed coat draped over his shoulders and wore a matching tweed "Deerstalker" hat.

He also carried a large pipe and a magnifying glass, in his coat pocket and made sure he carried both of these, everywhere he went. He did resemble Hermes in some ways, but was a lot younger than the old Professor.

Alfa felt that the floor of the tunnel was vibrating and assumed he was close to an underground station. He emerged through a drain at the corner of Marylebone Road and spotted a sign for Baker Street; his sense of direction was definitely much stronger.

He found the building numbered 221, which overlooked the crossroads, and was adjacent to Baker Street underground Station, so he knew he had found the correct place.

He spotted an opening at the side of the tall building and made his way down to the lower depths.

Slooth could hear someone coming and called out to Alfa, confirming that his cousin Hermes had already told him, that he would be visiting him.

After exchanging greetings, Slooth asked his new friend to join him in his humble abode.

They talked about the number of adventures that Alfa and the other dregs had undertaken, which interested Slooth, who was excited, after his cousin Hermes had wanted him to become involved

They got on very well and it seemed they'd known each other for a long time.

Slooth asked Alfa to take a look round his small abode, while he made some tea, but all Alfa could see were books and scraps of paper, that adorned the shelves, the floor and any spare surface.

During the refreshing tea-break, Slooth spoke of the conversation he had, with his cousin Hermes, but knew he was not to reveal where they were going, due to the evil Jinn trying to achieve the same goal, by intercepting any information.

Slooth escorted Alfa to another room at the rear of his lodgings, where he lifted up a dirty rug, then pointed to a trap door.

He lifted the wooden door and Alfa gasped at the sight before him.

Below the entrance was a very well-lit area and the faint sound of water, a long way down.

'What is this place Sooth,' Alfa enquired?

'Follow me down my friend, let me reveal what is below,' replied Slooth.

Alfa stood on a ledge and was instructed to use the ladder attached to it, then to keep descending, until he was at the very bottom.

After what seemed to be at least ten long minutes,

Alfa could see the base of the ladder and a vast expanse of water, which was an enormous underground lake, and was completely illuminated.

'Wow, this is something you don't see every day,' exclaimed Alfa.

'My dear young boy, *we* are in an underground reservoir, and the lake you can see before you, supply's the residents and businesses in central London with their water supplies.'

'Alfa, please take these, and place them into your ears', asked Slooth.

He had given Alfa a set of ear-plugs, as they were about to enter the enormous plant room, where the pumps and other important machinery were housed.

They followed a narrow corridor into the Plant Room; the noise was deafening, but Slooth pushed each of the ear-plugs further into Alfa's ears.

They continued further into the plant room, which eventually led to a long twisting passage.

Every thirty yards or so, there were a set of steps. Slooth explained that the steps were for the human Engineers to access the pumps and electrical components when required, in order to keep the water flowing, then eventually, once filtered, the water would be fit for drinking.

Alfa spotted a small dinghy moored to the side of the flowing water and suggested that they should use the craft, to take them to where they were going, as the tunnels looked endless.

Slooth gave Alfa a puzzled look!

The young dreg explained that they would need to access the Planetarium and the Waxworks and the

Dinghy would get them to these venues a lot quicker.

Once on board, Alfa waved his webbed hands above the water, which then became a fast-flowing stream.

The Dinghy sailed along the gushing current of water, assisted by the oars that Slooth had found laid on the boat's deck.

Alfa confirmed that the two places they sought, were below Marylebone Road, based on the "Stars and the Image of Man", the clues that had been revealed on the plaque, at St Pauls Cathedral.

'We are quite close my boy, stated Slooth. The entrances for both these places are just a few more yards away'.

Slooth grew more excited, the closer they got to the venues, even though he had been inside them, on many occasions.

They disembarked easily, after Alfa had slowed down the fast-moving current and tied the Dinghy to one of the rusty loops at the side of the underground stream.

'Did Hermes confirm what we were to look for at these two places Alfa? Asked Slooth.'

'I am afraid not my friend, I can only presume that my powers of deduction will assist us?'

'Ah, this is the place,' cried Slooth!

'I cannot see any means of access into the building Slooth, asked Alfa. How do we get in?'

'Elementary my dear Alfa, come with me!'

Slooth showed Alfa the edge of the Reservoir, which branched off into several different streams.

Alfa gazed across, at another amazing sight, something he had never seen before.

'I call this wonder of science, announced Slooth. This,

my boy, is a "Watervator"!'

Slooth explained that the constant flow of the stream was used, to power the steps upward, making them continuously going round!

'Step on my friend and jump when I say!' shouted Slooth.

The two comrades climbed onto the rotating watermill, before carefully jumping off, once they had reached the level required.

They stood side by side on the upper level and were confronted by two iron grids.

Both grids were identified with stencilled wording.

One stated "The Planetarium" and the other was "Madame Tussauds."

Slooth asked Alfa to choose which one he wanted to go to first.

'My senses tell me nothing Alfa stated, so let's start with the left-hand entrance!'

'To the Waxworks we go then', called Slooth!

Madame Tussauds was world renowned for its almost "Lifelike" wax models. The models, were copies of famous persons, old or young, together with "themed" sections, depicting life over the decades.

The waxworks were displayed throughout the building, and sometimes, were changed for newer models, depending on the interest shown by the people who wanted to see them.

The Waxworks was empty, except for the lifeless inhabitants!

Alfa and Slooth emerged from a Ventilation shaft and clambered down onto the exhibition floor.

'These models look very realistic Alfa, exclaimed

Slooth; almost as if they knew we were coming!'

Slooth removed his long pipe and magnifying glass from his coat pocket.

He placed the unlit pipe into his mouth and the glass to his right eye, which Alfa saw had grown extremely large.

'Now, we will unravel the secrets that are in this place; time for work,' stated Slooth!

Malus, the Jinn Master, had been observing the two dregs during their search below Marylebone Road and was about to unleash his cunning plan, once the time was right.

The Waxworks were very quiet and the exhibition hall held no clues for the two Detectives.so Alfa suggested that they split up and continue their search, but said he would remain in Telepathic contact at all times.

They separately carried on looking for any clues or any unusual items.

Alfa had just entered "The Chamber of Horrors", where he saw some very gruesome sights.

Slooth had entered "The Hall of Criminals", a place where he wanted to spend a lot of time, and promised himself that he would return soon.

He was carefully checking over the details, based on his interest of any criminal or associated subjects.

He was enamoured with the contents of the room, as he peered through his large magnifying glass.

He found a cabinet full of different weapons, and below a cluster of Guns and Knives, he noticed that they had been donated by an Inspector Gray of "Scotland

Yard".

Alfa walked around looking at the various exhibits and stopped at the Guillotine display, where he saw that some unfortunate person had lost his head, which was lying in a basket below the sharp blade.

He shivered at the thought, and moved on!

Slooth moved over to a cabinet adjacent to the Arsenal of Weapons and noticed an old batch of banknotes.

He read the wording below the paper money, which stated

"This Counterfeit Money was recovered from a foiled scam, at the Bank of England".

He pulled his magnifying glass closer and wondered why, if these notes were counterfeits, then why does only one of the notes have a motif printed onto it.

In the top right-hand corner, he saw that the motif was an open book.

Slooth wrote down all the details and thought it best to find Alfa, to discuss what he had found.

Alfa was still searching through the eerie exhibits in the Chamber of Horrors and started to feel quite cold, and assumed that the ghastly wax figures were to blame?

He stopped by a scene where there were three Witches standing around a bubbling cauldron. The three old hags looked as though they were about to cast a spell on some unfortunate person.

He continued his search for any clues and failed to notice that one of the witches was slowly moving.

'Alfa, Alfa, where are you, I think I have found something interesting, where are you?'

Alfa's concentration suddenly broke.

He spotted the moving witch, who then pulled away.

He saw the face, who wore a black cloak and pointed hat. It was the ugly sight of Malus!

Then Alfa suddenly disappeared!

'I, Malus, the Prince of Curses, have sent the miserable dreg to the "Bastille of Pain"!'

Slooth tried to hide behind a wax model of the Frankenstein monster, but Malus demanded that he show himself.

. *'Go and tell your dreg infidels, that the Jinn have captured Alfa, go now!'*

Slooth made his way back through the reservoir, the noisy pump room and back to the tunnels, on his way to Russell Square.

Hermes was saddened to hear such bad news, and vowed to find a way to get his friend back, but was worried about the Bastille of Pain, a place that he had learned, was not a very nice place to be!

He then went over to his secret room, to look for something to help him.

Slooth sat in his cousin's chair, removed his magnifying glass and studied the details he had written down from the banknote at the waxworks.

Hermes then returned from his secret room, with an arm full of charts and drawings.

'Malus must have grown tired of the evil forces being defeated by the Dregs; this was probably why he decided to go to the Waxworks himself; as his intentions were, no doubt, to capture Alfa!'

The worried Professor asked Slooth for the details he had taken from the waxworks and for a brief moment, he forgot about his friend, who was now in the Bastille.

'This banknote has revealed only one clue my dear

Slooth, but I feel there is something missing, we must return to the waxworks and continue the search!'

Hermes and Slooth joined hands and materialised in the "Chamber of Horrors".

Malus summoned his evil forces and told them that he had sent one of the dregs to the Bastille of Pain, and confirmed how easy it was to beat their foe.

He ordered Asper to go to the waxwork museum, to get the banknote with the open book in one corner, which could be found in the display, inside the "Hall of Criminals".

Hermes and Slooth walked away from the scene of Alfas disappearance, and the old wizard remembered the words from the plaque from the St Pauls Cathedral.

'When the Stars meet the images of man!' Which he kept repeating to himself!

Slooth remarked that they had to choose from two entrances, when he and Alfa had disembarked from the Dinghy.

'I think Alfa may have chosen the wrong one, my dear cousin,' said Slooth!

'Good thinking Slooth, we will try the other entrance, but be aware, that the Jinn could still be watching us!'

The two dregs entered the right-hand ventilation shaft, but didn't notice the evil presence of Asper, making his way through the ventilation shaft of the left-hand grid.

The shaft behind the right-hand entrance, led to a short tunnel and some steps. At the top of the steps, the two dregs spotted a doorway.

'Look Slooth, above the door!' Said the old wizard.

Hermes had spotted a sign, showing an arrow pointing left for Madame Tussauds and another arrow pointing right, for the Planetarium.

He opened the door that led to the Planetarium, and they both entered. Behind the door was a box containing some keys, which had been marked as spare keys, for Madame Tussauds; Slooth used his magnifying glass to check each one.

He stated that there was a hook without a key and a piece of paper had been placed over the hook, which he removed, and read out the contents.

'The Key to the Cabinet of Weapons is held at Scotland Yard!'

Hermes thought about the words and stated that they already had the details from the banknote, but now there was a key to the weapons cabinet, at Scotland Yard.

Slooth continued to search for other clues, but Hermes asked him to call it a day, stating that it was getting late.

He thanked his cousin for his invaluable assistance, but Slooth apologised for not getting to Alfa in time.

'Goodbye for now my dear cousin, I will contact you soon.'

Hermes vanished from the Planetarium and re-appeared at his home in Russell Square.

Alfa was trapped in "The Bastille of Pain", a place of punishment for the evil Jinn. He heard a voice call out behind him, who noticed the dreg, and wanted to know why he was there.

'I am Alfa, I was sent here by Malus!' Confirmed the brave dreg.

Alfa looked out of his cell, but couldn't see anyone.

The evil force laughed and confirmed his name as Korpos, who had also been sent there by the "Prince of Curses", his evil Master, for certain reasons.

'Tell me Korpos, do you have any powers here!'

Alfa wondered whether he could trick this Jinn prisoner, and help him to escape.

'My powers are limited in this place, why do you ask!'

Alfa kept silent, but Korpos in anger stated that he was tired of being in the Bastille; and of Malus, so he informed the young dreg that he would be sent to a place where he could be seen, but could not be heard!

Korpos laughed as Alfa suddenly disappeared.

Hermes had a strange feeling inside and felt that Alfa had returned, but where was he?

Malus summoned Korpos and asked him for an explanation.

'Why did you expel the Dreg from the Bastille, asked Malus, *and where have you sent him?'*

Korpos explained that he was annoyed with the dreg and had sent the boy to a place known as "Millbank"!

'Maybe you were right to send him away, said Malus; the dregs will have sensed he is back, so they will have to search for him and this will give us time to find the clue from the banknote!'

Korpos was sent to Millbank, to watch over the young dreg and to report on anything that was of interest.

The Jinn forces were trying to decipher the clue of the open book on the counterfeit banknote. Asper advised his master that there was something missing.

Hermes went to Chelsea Barracks to see his old friend Rank and asked him to assist him with something of great importance.

'You're familiar with Scotland Yard my friend, can you please take me there, so that we can find a key, a key that will open up a weapons cabinet at Madame Tussauds.

Rank expressed his thanks to his old friend, for asking him to assist him, and stood to attention.

Malus had watched them from his evil quarters and had overheard the conversation.

'So, the dregs are to visit the building of the Policemen, I will have to arrange a welcoming committee to greet them!'

Korpos had arrived at a building in Millbank; the famous Tate Gallery.

The great rooms within the Gallery housed many famous works of Art. In one particular room, there was a painting depicting a battle scene.

The battle was taking place outside the walls of a castle; with the gruesome artwork detailing the knights fighting with their enemies.

Watching from the castle tower stood a lonely figure, it was Alfa!

11: THE OLD DREG OF THREADNEEEDLE STREET.

'So, here we are Rank, confirmed Hermes. Above us is the Old Scotland Yard Building, that was used many years ago!'

Hermes and Rank had travelled via Whitehall, to locate the famous building, once renowned for housing the Policemen of London.

'It was very clever of you Rank, to inform me that the key we seek, would be in this building, and not in the New Scotland Yard premises, in St James Street!'

Rank, in his military manner, informed Hermes that he was just doing his duty.

The tunnels below Old Scotland Yard were dark and musty; the old prison cells, once occupied, were now vacant.

Rank informed Hermes that they would find the old Key House, beyond the gates ahead.

The gates were locked, but Hermes grabbed his old friend's hand, and they found themselves on the other side.

They found the Key House, which was in a large cupboard along the corridor.

The cupboard contained several old filing cabinets, which Rank wished he had the time to check out, but time was of the essence!

Rank opened the unlocked Key Box and checked the old rusty keys contained inside, which were covered in cobwebs. He took out a piece of cardboard and blew away the silky mesh.

'Key one *Sir*, which is the spare key to the Bloody Tower!'

Hermes asked Rank to address him by name, not in military style, stating that he was not in the army now!

'What was the key number for the Weapons Cabinet you found at Madame Tussaud's Rank?'

'Ah, here we are Sir, sorry, I mean Hermes, it is Key number Thirty-Three, the Key to the Cabinet of Arms!'

Hermes located the hook and noticed there were two keys.

One had some wording engraved onto it.

He passed the rusty old key to Rank, who read out the wording.

'Property of the Bank of England.'

Hermes was certain that this was the clue they had been looking for, his instincts were normally accurate.

He also recalled the counterfeit banknote with the open book.

'Rank my friend, we will make our way to Threadneedle Street, to the Bank of England, but first, I will contact my uncle, who just happens to live quite close to the building.'

Rank tidied up the rusty keys and firmly closed the box, while Hermes was telepathically contacting his uncle Wadd.

He wondered whether his aging relative would respond.

The telepathy worked, and he had made contact with his uncle.

He had not seen Wadd for a long time and knew they had a lot to discuss.

'My dear nephew Hermes, how are you, what can I do for you, it has been such a long time!'

Hermes briefly explained the situation to Wadd and stated that he and Rank, would join him in the vicinity of the Bank of England.

The two friends left Old Scotland Yard in Whitehall, and made their way down to the tunnels below, following the underground route via Westminster, then through the tunnels and gulley's, below the City of London and towards Bank Station.

In their haste, although Rank had managed to tidy up the Key Box, they were missing one item, the other key on hook thirty-three; a key that opened something at the Bank of England!

The streets above Bank Station were busy, with the usual public going about their business, either to their place of work, or, if they had worked at night, to return back home to sleep.

Above them, Hermes and Rank could hear a voice shouting strange words at the passers-by. It didn't matter what he was saying, as the humans were giving him coins for the daily papers he was selling.

They had arranged to meet Wadd at his home below

Threadneedle Street and had found their way through a tunnel, which took them into a room, where all the walls were covered in foreign currency.

'Far too many banknotes' Hermes muttered, to himself.

Wadd was old but still active for his age. Any powers he used to have, he assumed, were no longer working, probably due to not using them?

Wadd was one of the Elders; he wore a blue pin-striped suit, together with a white collared shirt and red tie. He also wore a blue waistcoat with a bolder stripe than the design on his suit, with a Fob watch and gold chain, inside one of the pockets.

He had already laid out his medals, knowing that he was expecting company, but decided to pin them onto his jacket. Walking these days, for Wadd, was becoming quite difficult, so he had to use a walking stick, to assist him with his balance.

Rank and Hermes had arrived at the old Veteran's home. Rank admired the row of medals pinned to his suit and complemented Wadd over them.

'My dear Hermes, so good to see you and also nice to see you again Rank, it's been a very long time'.

Wadd had some tea and biscuits available and invited his visitors to take a seat.

The three dreg elders enthusiastically spoke of the past, of the other elders and many more subjects, whilst consuming their tea and biscuits, but Hermes had to interrupt his dear uncle, stating that time was ticking away and there were some very important issues to address.

Hermes produced the key taken from the cabinet at

155

Old Scotland Yard and passed it over to his uncle.

Wadd confirmed that he had seen this type of key before, and was certain that it was probably used to open some of the cupboards or some rooms for Antiques.

'Did you hear that', Hermes asked his uncle?

Both Wadd and Rank could not hear anything, but assumed that the noise was possibly above them, on Threadneedle Street.

Hermes thought he could hear a cry for help, he could make out a faint voice, but it was not too clear.

He tried to visualise what, or who was trying to contact him, but something was obscuring his inner visions, although he thought he heard the word "Bank"?

Wadd asked his nephew if he could help, but Hermes confirmed again, that all he had heard, was the word "Bank".

'Come, let us see if there is anyone calling me from above us, stated Hermes; let's go to the Bank and see if we can find the room that this key will open!'

As they made their way into the Bank of England, Hermes was confused as to why anyone would be calling him from there, but was hoping they would find out, once they had found their way inside.

Hermes noticed that his uncle was a lot older and was finding it difficult to keep up with them, so he asked them to join hands.

They immediately arrived into a corridor, where the doors were marked "Storage".

Wadd had been here before, and his energy seemed to have returned.

He confirmed to his two companions that the far room on the right-hand side, was where the Antiques were stored.

Hermes placed the key into the lock, turned the key. The door opened.

All three of them were astounded at the sights before them, the room was full of paintings, furniture and numerous Antiques.

Hermes suggested that they each pick a different corner to start their search and to look for anything unusual and somehow related to their lost book.

It was all peace and quiet in the world of the Jinn. Malus had instructed Asper to be ready at short notice, for his call. The "Prince of Curses" watched with interest, the activities inside the Bank of England, hoping that the dregs would solve the clues for him.

Hermes and Rank looked at Wadd, who was studying a very unusual box he had removed from a glass cabinet.

'Here nephew, please take a look at this box, asked Wadd. It has a familiar design on the front!'

Wadd was certain he had seen it before somewhere?

Hermes placed an index finger over his lips, advising his companions, that someone was possibly listening to their conversation.

'This casket has no means of access,' stated Wadd, as he passed it over to Hermes.

The old Wizard placed a finger over a raised section of the box; the box suddenly sprang open, causing him to drop it on the floor.

A Shaft of light emitted from the open container, then a three-dimensional scene appeared.

Wadd started to question his nephew, but Hermes

quickly gestured him to stay quiet.

The three-dimensional vision was set in a large room, which was empty, except for an oak desk and two flags.

Hermes confirmed that these were the "Stars and Stripes"; the flag of the United States of America!

The scene became cloudy and vanished, the shaft of light returned to the box, which then closed.

'This room with the American Flags; I have seen this somewhere before,' called Rank!

Hermes asked Rank to wait until later, when they could talk about it without somebody eavesdropping, then waved his hands over it, to ensure it would be safe from the Jinn.

Malus had seen enough; he summoned Asper and gave him his orders, and asking him to be ready, in preparation for their next move.

Hermes and Rank made sure Wadd had got home safely and, after a short while, said his farewell, and promised him they would see him soon.

Rank saluted the old dreg of Threadneedle Street; Wadd saluted back.

Hermes and Rank made their way to Chelsea Barracks. On their way, the Professor heard the cries again, only this time, he saw the name of a road.

'It was not Bank I heard earlier, he exclaimed to a puzzled looking Rank, it was "Millbank"!'

Rank wondered what the old Professor was talking about, but Hermes remained silent.

'Come Rank, we have an appointment in Pimlico!'

Rank couldn't believe it; so much action in one day!

Malus and Asper were now together, Asper eagerly awaited his masters wishes.

'You will go to the place called the "Tate Gallery", which you will find in Millbank!'

'Once you arrive there, you will join Korpos and, together, you will find the old Professor and the dreg they call Rank!'

'Do not fail me again!', Malus called out!

Hermes and Rank had arrived at their destination; the Tate Gallery, which overlooked the river Thames.

It was getting quite late, so it was closed. All the visitors and Tourists had departed, so the Gallery, thankfully, would be quiet.

Once inside, they both had a good look round, to see if they could hear any cries for help, but everywhere was deserted and silent.

Hermes suggested that they should go to the upper rooms, as he sensed that this was the place to look.

As they got closer to the upper rooms, Hermes could hear the cries, and confirmed to Rank that they were in the right area, but to be vigilant, during the search!

Korpos had been warned by Malus to expect the two dregs, and that Asper would also accompany him, at some stage.

The upper Gallery was very cold. The professor stated that they should make their search together, as he was certain the Jinn were quite close.

They looked at the paintings on the walls, searching for any clues, then they stopped at a large Mural and studied the scene closely.

It was a painting of a Castle, with a Battle in full flow outside the walls. Hermes produced a large magnifying glass from his coat pocket and passed it over to Rank.

The painting was large, but the figures looked very small.

Rank, the old Veteran, scanned the glass over the soldiers who were locked in battle, but was sure he could see something moving from within the Castle.

Hermes looked at other paintings in the same vicinity, but noticed a shape moving towards him and shouted to Rank, to hold the Magnifying Glass as high as he could.

The puzzled old soldier did as he was told.

As he held the glass towards the roof, he became protected by a "Force-Field"!

Korpos moved closer and spoke to Hermes. The old Professor could only hear the voice, as the Jinn warrior was invisible.

'So, Dreg, is that the best you can do, a Force-Field cannot keep me out!'

Hermes sensed the presence of another force and reached into his other coat pocket, then addressed the invisible forces.

'You have taken Alfa from us; do as we say and bring him back!'

As he was shouting out to the Jinn warriors, he had produced the box they had found at the Bank of England.

He laid the box on the floor, touched the top and a shaft of light appeared.

Korpos laughed and told the old Professor that his feeble powers could not harm the Jinn.

Rank, who had been sucked into the Force-Field, was unable to move or do anything to help his friend.

Hermes moved away from the box, which produced a scene, that interested Korpos.

The scene showed Korpos together with his Master, Malus. They were both arguing over something. Korpos became angry and called out.

'How did you come by this box dreg; this belongs to the Jinn!'

Korpos reached out to snatch the box and was physically thrown against a wall, leaving him stunned and helpless.

Asper was fuming and called out!

'So, we meet again dregs, and you are still using your useless trickery; Korpos was weak, but I am not!'

Hermes recognised the voice of the invisible Asper; he remembered the duel in the "Whispering Gallery", but this time, he did not have a mirror!

'Dregs, you cannot defeat me; surrender, or I will use our evil powers against you all!'

Hermes looked at the box; could it be used again?

. *'You have no powers left old man – Surrender, NOW!'*

Aspers hideous form materialised; his eyes beckoned to Hermes.

'Look at me dreg, look at me now!'

The old Wizard felt his strength weakening fast, there was nothing he could do; he could feel his bowed head slowly beginning to rise.

'No, said the old wizard; No, I must be strong!'

Rank called out from inside the force-field, but he still couldn't be heard.

The two pairs of eyes were almost level, Rank shouted again, but Hermes was now in a Hypnotic state.

It was too late!

All of a sudden, a small metal object hit Asper, it was a Key!

Asper immediately vanished.

Hermes awoke from his Hypnotic trance and glanced over at Rank, who was still contained within the force-field.

He then spotted Wadd.

'My dear uncle, it was you who came to my rescue!'

'Yes, my dear nephew, I sensed you were in danger and quickly made my way here.'

Wadd owned up, stating that he forgot to replace the key at the Bank of England.

He had been thinking about the events at the Bank, when he remembered about the key.

He also explained that his intuition told him of the danger everyone was in, and remembered that he still had some of his powers, albeit very rusty.

The force-field was removed and Rank, who quickly saluted Wadd, explained that he was helpless within the shield, but thanked Hermes for the protection.

'Now, we must get back to the paintings, said the old professor. I feel that we were very close to spotting something, before we were so rudely interrupted by the Jinn!'

The three dregs went over to inspect the artwork, then the veteran soldier continued looking at the battle scene he was looking at earlier, and spotted something straight away.

He pointed at a figure in one of the towers.

It was Alfa!

Rank called the two dregs over and pointed at the

figure in the tower. Hermes touched the painting and could sense nothing; all he could think of, was how was he going to get his young apprentice out!

Hermes knew that his powers were weak, further to their earlier incident with the Jinn.

He expressed his sadness to his colleagues and apologised for not being able to release the trapped young dreg, but glanced over at the box, hoping that it would work, for a third time.

He explained to his fellow dregs that these types of boxes could normally be used, up to three times, but not to be to upset, if it wouldn't work again!

'If there is a slim chance to release Alfa, then we must try, stated the old wizard, to his companions!'

Hermes had read about the box, and its magical powers, in the "Book of Dreg civilisation"!

He touched the lid once more, Alfa suddenly appeared and the box vanished.

'Welcome back my dear friend, we are so glad to see you back!'

Alfa thanked the Professor and Rank, for releasing him, stating that the tower had become a prison and that it was the most terrifying experience he'd ever had; even scarier than the Bastille of Pain!

Hermes made sure that the young dreg was alright and told him that his uncle, was his saviour.

Alfa thanked the old dreg of Threadneedle Street with a tight handshake and also thanked him, for helping the dregs in their continuing quest.

'We must leave now, called Hermes. Our job is finished here.'

Hermes said goodbye to his uncle after they had left

the Tate Gallery. Rank asked if he could go back to Threadneedle Street with Wadd, as he wanted to discuss some military tactics.

After saying their goodbyes, Alfa and Hermes transported themselves to the room below the British Museum.

'It appears that the Jinn are watching our every move Alfa, so from now on, we must be more alert, we must also communicate, only by telepathy, hoping that the Jinn will not be able to hear our thoughts.

'Come Alfa, I have something to show you.'

They entered the secret room.

The room was fitted with heavy soundproofed doors, and, once inside, the heavy doors closed and they were able to discuss the next phase of their quest, without any hindrance.

'Now my boy, we have to think about the two identical flags that came from a vision'.

Hermes explained to Alfa, that his uncle Wadd had found the box, in one of the rooms in the Bank of England.

'I have already done some research over this my boy, and my thoughts have revealed that we should seek a building with a Golden Eagle above it, overlooking a large square?'

Alfa searched his memory, knowing that he had seen this building before.

'The building we seek with the two flags and the Eagle, said Hermes, is in Grosvenor Square, London. It is the American Embassy, and we must send someone there; possibly a Diplomat.?'

Hermes suggested that they must find someone who

can be trusted, and assist them, when we try to find the clues, we need. And, most of all someone who is not afraid of the Jinn!

The cunning old Wizard and his apprentice, began to put together a masterplan, before the next quest, at the American Embassy.

12: A DIPLOMAT IN GROSVENOR SQUARE.

Malus, the "Prince of Curses" summoned his evil forces to his side.

'Again, you have been defeated by these weak dregs, they are making fools of you all!'

Malus had the complete attention of his assembled apostles, and began to vent his anger at each of them.

'Korpos, you were fooled by a box and Asper, you were beaten by a rusty key!'

Tavet and Belua smirked at their failed colleagues.

'SILENCE!' Shouted Malus.

The echoes of his voice boomed all over the world of the Jinn, in Inferus, the dark lands.

The band of evil knights were now trembling and awaiting their fate!

Malus looked at each one of his evil warriors and confirmed that *he* was the only one who could deal with the Jinn's enemy.

He asked them all to leave, and ordered them each, to come up with a solution, one that would ensure victory, or alternatively, they would be severely punished.

Kalor was released from the Bastille of Pain and was asked to join with the other four dejected Jinn forces.

Malus gave him the same lecture, stating that the five of them should be able to come up with a plan, a plan that would ensure they could get to the Book of Dreg civilisation, before the dregs could find it.

The five evil warriors sat in the "Chamber of Silence", with each one trying to come up with a plot to overthrow the dregs.

Malus kept watch on the debate, but was annoyed that he was unable to hear anything.

Hermes and Alfa were discussing their next move, and hoped that the sound-proofed secret room would protect their plans.

Hermes stressed that they must address their current security, as they were getting much closer to their goal, and decided that only the two of them would communicate with each other by telepathy, when they were outside, during their quests, and to gradually teach, or advise their dreg friends the skill, to ensure it was used properly.

'And now my dear Alfa, the Plan!'

Alfa listened carefully, when the old professor started to unravel his strategy.

'Somebody will need to get into the American Embassy undetected, but whoever we choose, said the wise old sage, will need to understand that the situation is becoming more dangerous, due to the Jinn being frustrated over their constant failures!'

Alfa volunteered straight away; Hermes knew he

would. They spoke of the mission, and Hermes reiterated the current mood of the Jinn, and that they would use every evil power they possessed, to try and defeat them.

Alfa expressed his agreement, knowing he would need to be more vigilant.

'Remember Alfa, when we leave this room, only you and I will know the Plan!'

The Plan of Action was for someone to enter the American Embassy, someone who would know that every move would be watched by the Jinn, but to use their strengths to create one or more diversions, when required.

'This "Decoy", continued the old wizard, will have to lead the Jinn on a false trail, allowing time for you Alfa, to gather the clues, in the room of the Flags.'

Alfa liked the plan and couldn't wait to get started!

'Who can we trust Alfa, who would be the best candidate to undertake this dangerous task?'

Alfa suggested that Levi would be a good choice, due to his manner and ability.

'A wise decision my boy, exclaimed Hermes, Levi will be our Diplomat. We will need to give him something to take to the Embassy; something that will become a distraction, to the Jinn!'

'I am glad I chose correctly, thought Alfa!'

'Now go to the embassy my young warrior, I will contact Levi and advise him of his mission!'

The Golden Eagle sat perched on the roof, above the American Embassy; it overlooked the green patches of grass, in the walled gardens of Grosvenor Square.

The "Bald" Eagle above the building, constantly kept its eyes, on the Embassy and its residents and also watched the people, who used the gardens below, for their recreation.

Grosvenor Square was very quiet, the roads and adjoining streets were almost deserted. The pigeons and squirrels in the gardens, roamed free to search the litter bins that had not been emptied, and helping themselves to the various scraps of food, just waiting to be eaten.

The Embassy was beginning to get quite busy, and just inside the main doors, there were two Security Guards, who were each armed, with a handgun and rifle, and looked as though they wouldn't tolerate any nonsense from anyone.

At the left-hand side, of the embassy, a small queue of people waited patiently, ready to apply for their Visa's, which would allow them to visit the USA.

On the first floor, there was a very large room, with white painted walls, which was the office of the American Ambassador. The room was quite large, but only had a single, large table, two chairs and an oak desk, which all sat on a plush red carpet, making the white walls look like a shade of pink, when the sun shone through.

The solid Oak desk, had a mass of files and papers on top of it, which were kept in place by a large glass paperweight. Behind the desk, there was a framed portrait of the current President of the USA, with an identical Red, White and Blue flag, on each side of the Portrait, known as the "Stars and Stripes".

Levi had welcomed the call from Hermes and made his way to Russell Square, in record time. Hermes had given Levi a book, which contained instructions on the first page, that should only be read after he was inside the Embassy.

'Once you have entered the American Embassy, explained Hermes, carefully read the detailed information on the first page, but on no account, must you reveal these words to anyone!'

Levi didn't have to be reminded that the evil forces of the Jinn would probably be watching his every move!'

Malus addressed Kalor.

'Kalor, it is time to go; go to Grosvenor Square and seek the dreg with the book, but watch only, until I give you further instructions, remember, do *nothing* until I contact you!'

'As you command my lord,' Kalor replied.

Levi headed through the tunnels and gulley's, from Russell Square and followed the underground stations via Holborn, Leicester Square and Green Park.

He finally surfaced in Upper Brook Street, on the edge of Grosvenor Square and made his way into the lower depths of the Embassy.

Alfa was close by, but had to make sure he could not be seen by his friend Levi.

Kalor was already inside the Embassy, he was determined not to fail his master again, knowing that he would be returned to the Bastille of Pain; but this time, it could possibly be forever!

Levi found his way into the underground Car Park and had opened up the book that Hermes had given him.

The old Professor's writing was clear and precise, which he read carefully and followed the instructions.

'Go to the stairway and find your way to the first

floor. As you look down the corridor, locate the room marked Visas. Enter this room and go to the bookshelves!'

Levi followed the directions and located the bookshelves.

'Look at the third shelf up and there you will find an empty space!'

Malus looked down at the dreg with excitement, hoping that the Jinn would be victorious, this time.

'Place your book in this empty space and remove the book, to the left of the space!'

Everything went according to plan; Levi now had the second book in his possession.

Malus was intrigued and warned Kalor to be ready for the dregs next move.

Alfa slipped into the Ambassador's office quietly and undetected, hoping that Levi was following the details he had been given by Hermes.

Levi opened up the second book and read the contents on the first page, as instructed.

'Look at the fourth shelf above you and find the book entitled "Lunar Landscapes", do not touch the book, keep on looking at it and await my signal!'

Levi recalled the briefing from Hermes asking him to do as he was instructed and nothing else!

Kalor changed his appearance and had turned into a fly. Levi looked up and saw the fly buzzing around the bookshelves, but his senses were not strong enough yet, to suspect that it was a Jinn warrior.

Alfa was searching the Ambassadors office for clues and saw a glass paperweight, on top of the papers. He lifted the weight and turned it over, to read the words.

"A Gift from the Theatre Royal, Drury Lane".

The young dreg stared hard at the heavy object, making the words disappear.

He then placed the paperweight into a small pouch, tied to his belt.

Hermes spoke to Levi telepathically and asked him to remove the fifth book from the same shelf.

The bookcase started to revolve, creaking as it turned; then Levi awaited his next command.

Hermes placed Levi into a trance, and asked him to follow his directions.

'Follow the path that leads to the black door, turn the handle and enter the room, then wait for my further instructions!'

Levi did as he was told, the fly followed and watched with interest.

Malus sensed that something was not right and quickly made a scan of other rooms in the Embassy.

He spotted the room with the two flags and knew he had seen it before.

He remembered seeing the vision from the box, at the Bank of England.

'Kalor, find the room with the two flags, hurry, we have been tricked!'

Kalor flew out of the room and made his way to the first floor, where he found the Ambassador's room and the two flags.

'Turn around and leave the room', Hermes instructed the hypnotised Levi; turn right and go to the Chamber!'

Levi continued to follow the old wizard's words and found his way into the Chamber. As he entered, he was confronted by an ugly sight, Kalor had changed back to his usual ugly form.

'Tell me dreg, what is in this room, what have you found?'

Levi was still in a trance, then a voice spoke, with the words coming from *his* mouth.

It was the voice of Hermes.

*'The person here present, speaks for the dreg people, and we know that the Jinn intend to steal our sacred book, but we can tell you now, the book is **not** in this building!'*

Alfa heard the voice of Hermes, and went to investigate, finding his way into the empty chamber, where Levi stood.

Kalor heard someone coming and changed his shape once more.

Kalor was now a large wolf, and was standing in front of Levi.

Then the voice of the old professor spoke again.

'It's no use trying to destroy this person, shouted Hermes, *your powers are of no use in this room!'*

The wolf leapt towards Levi, but was met with a nasty shock.

An invisible force-field had been placed around Levi. The wolf howled; he was in pain!

Hermes repeated himself: *'Your powers are useless here!'* Hermes had turned the room into a Neutral Zone.

Malus was angered, he quickly sent a flash of lightning into the room, then Alfa entered, holding the glass paperweight.

The lightning bolt hit the force-field, which then bounced off and hit the paperweight, causing a vision to appear.

The vision revealed something that startled Alfa.

A bright halo appeared within the vision and at the centre, was the "Book of Dreg civilisations"!

Alfa clearly saw the book, but the Wolf's paw had reached out to it, making the vision disappear.

During the incident, inside the chamber, Alfa hadn't noticed that he had dropped the paperweight, which Kalor spotted, and had placed it inside his cloak.

Kalor was summoned to return to the Dark Lands, by Malus, who asked him to describe everything he had seen. Kalor could only confirm that he had seen the book of dreg civilisation, within the vision.

'So, said the Prince of Curses, it seems that the dregs have another clue, a clue as to the location of their book.

Malus was now convinced, that Levi had been put there as a decoy, to throw them off the scent.

Kalor then produced the glass object, stating that he had managed to retrieve the item, which was dropped by the young dreg.

Malus took the paperweight and carefully inspected it, then called Kalor a fool, and threw the glass weight across the floor, which smashed into several pieces.

Kalor looked at the fragments on the floor and spotted some words.

'My lord, said Kalor, I can see some faint words on the glass; I can make out two of them, "Drury and Theatre"?'

Malus for once, was apologetic and stated that these words, had identified the Theatre Royal in Drury Lane, and called upon his evil soldiers to join them in his room.

'Kalor has managed to find the next clue, stated Malus. We now know where to search, but before this, has any of you managed to come up with a plan?'

Tavet spoke first and proposed that they concentrate on the young dreg called Alfa, and that he should be brought to the dark lands, to be imprisoned, with no means of an escape.

'A good plan Tavet, but you have had many opportunities to seize the boy, all without success!'

'And you Belua?'

Malus looked over at his evil warrior, whose plan was to capture each dreg one by one, then to shrink them all and place them into a bottle, where they would be his trophies.

'Good Belua, exclaimed Malus. It is now clearer that we all understand the importance of capturing the dregs!'

Asper was asked next by Malus.to reveal his thoughts and looking more devious than ever, Asper suggested that now they knew the details of where the dregs will be going next and we also know that they usually call upon their fellow dregs to assist them....

'Yes, yes, we know all of this, get to the point Asper!' Shouted an impatient Malus.

'I propose to take the form of one of the dregs and this way, I can actually be present when they make their next move!'

Malus was happy with Asper, for devising such a cunning plan.

He then turned to Korpos, who had been waiting patiently and stated that he had heard enough.

'We have much to do, my warriors, now go, and be triumphant; and Korpos, we will speak later, once we have been to the Theatre!'

He then dismissed the Jinn Warriors, after giving each of them their orders.

Alfa and Levi were sitting inside the secret room below the British Museum, running through the events at the Embassy.

Hermes asked Alfa to confirm everything about the Embassy, and became excited when Alfa had seen the lost book, within the vision.

'All I can remember seeing before it vanished, said Alfa, was two large iron girders, which were pointing upwards; sorry Professor, there was not enough time to study the vision in greater detail!'

Hermes stated that he would consult his charts, to see if there was any evidence of the two girders.

'Levi, my brave fellow, called Hermes. I am sorry but I have not had time to congratulate you on your Diplomatic assistance at the Embassy!'

Levi shrugged his shoulders; he felt very proud of himself, for doing a good job.

'A job well done, Levi, I hope you have recovered and have no after effects from being placed into the trance?'

Levi could not remember being in a trance, but assured Hermes, that he was OK.

The old Professor then suggested that Levi prepare some food and drink for himself and that others would join them shortly. Hermes apologised, but said he needed to discuss something with Alfa.

The old wizard did not want to risk too many people knowing about the next stage of their quest.

'Now, Alfa, we now know that the book is close, so it

is of great importance that we get to Drury Lane.'

Alfa then remembered he had lost the paperweight, when he was confronted by Kalor.

'Which is why we must get there as quickly as possible!' Advised the cunning old wizard, after hearing Alfa's thoughts.

Alfa confirmed that the Jinn maybe unable to see the words under the paperweight, but Hermes told him not to underestimate the desperate evil forces.

Levi knocked on the Metal door of the soundproofed room and stated that Dombey and Webley had arrived.

Hermes and Alfa left the secret room and welcomed their two good friends.

'Just in time my good friends, stated Hermes. Please help yourselves with something to eat!'

Dombey couldn't wait!

Webley asked Alfa if there was any progress regarding the lost book; but Alfa didn't respond.

Levi narrated the details of their quest at the American Embassy, which left Dombey very impressed at his heroics, about becoming a Diplomat in Grosvenor Square.

Knowing there were many things to discuss, the old Professor thanked Levi for his valuable assistance at the embassy and stated that he had to finalise some other plans, with his colleagues.

Levi expressed his understanding and stated that he was always available. The Ex-Diplomat explained that he had already arranged to meet up with Float.

The old wizard knew Levi wanted to relate the exciting events of his recent exploits, to his friend.

Back inside the Professors secret room, the four dregs

were planning their next moves.

'Gentlemen, we are now confident that the lost book is close by, Alfa please continue.'

'We will shortly be going to the Theatre Royal in Drury Lane, advised Alfa; and Hermes will be accompanying us on this occasion. The Jinn are probably aware that we are so near to finding our book and every effort must be made, to ensure our safety.'

Dombey and Webley listened intently, to their good friend.

'It will, therefore, be in all our interests, said Alfa, to restrict any information to just Hermes and myself!'

Both Dombey and Webley agreed and Alfa asked the Professor to continue.

'I have a relative who resides close to the Theatre, confirmed the professor. My cousin Dame will assist us, and it will be good to see her after so many years.'

Hermes explained that his cousin had lived by the Theatre for a long time and had contacted her recently, to confirm that he, and a few friends would visit her quite soon.

Malus summoned Asper to his chamber and confirmed that he had an important task for him, which involved a visit to the Theatre.

13: BEHIND THE MASQUE.

It was cold heading through the underground tunnels, when the four comrades were making their way from Russell Square; moving faster than normal, and heading for Drury Lane, in west-central London.

It was very busy above them, with more traffic than ever ploughing their way through to different parts of the city, or to other destinations, depending on which bridge the vehicles chose to cross.

Hermes grew more excited as they got closer to the Theatre. Was it the thought of getting the lost book back, or was it because he was going to see his cousin Dame?

Asper was already inside the Theatre, searching the area by the Stage Door, to see if he could find any clues, but to no avail.

He then followed some wooden stairs down to the lower level, which was just below the stage.

He could hear the sound of someone humming a tune, and found his way to the stage, to investigate.

He hid behind a rail of brightly coloured costumes and

watched the lady dreg, searching through one of the other clothing racks and humming to herself, as she looked.

It was Dame, the cousin of Hermes.

Dame wore a long, flowing purple dress, with a black shiny belt around her waist. She also wore a headband with a single flower resting beneath it, looking as though she was about to go on stage

Asper knew that the dregs were on their way to meet her, so he stayed in his hiding place behind the costume rail, waiting for their arrival.

Alfa confirmed to everyone, that they were close to the Theatre, and to be on their guard.

The four figures emerged from a drain, close to the Stage Door, and made their way inside.

Hermes reminded everyone again, warning them all, to be *extra* vigilant and to stay close to him, in the event of meeting any unwelcome visitors.

'My dear cousin Dame, how are you?' Called Hermes.

'Hermes, it is lovely to see you after such a long time, I am very well, thank you for asking.'

Three silent dregs waited patiently, but were finally introduced to Dame.

Webley felt embarrassed and decided to take a quick gulp of his medicine, then let out a very loud burp!

'Alfa, Hermes has told me all about you and how you are leading the quest for our lost book; it is so good to meet you, and your friends!'

'And you must be Webley.' Dame assumed. How nice to see you too, you are very sweet.'

Webley felt very embarrassed, his face turned red.

Dombey bowed before Dame, who expressed how

honoured she was for such a polite greeting.

After everyone had offered their greetings, Dame led her guests to a room, below the stage.

Asper moved away from his hiding place and made sure he could hear everyone, once they had entered the room.

Hermes explained to his cousin, what had occurred during the visit to the American Embassy, and of the glass paperweight, with the Theatre details on its base.

Dame assumed that the glass paperweight was probably a gift to the Ambassador, when he attended one of the many shows.

Alfa asked if the object was unique, and whether it was purposely made for the Ambassadors visit, but Dame responded and confirmed that the gift shop, in the main foyer was full of them.

Both Hermes and Alfa started to assume that they were on a wild goose chase.

'What about the vision, where I saw the lost book?' Alfa asked quizzically; but Hermes didn't reply.

Webley realised he had left his medicine by the Stage Door and made his way out quietly, to retrieve it, but nobody seemed to notice the small dreg leaving the room.

As he picked up the bottle, Asper moved towards him and, with a swift hand gesture, he had changed into Webley. Asper checked himself in a mirror close by, and agreed that nobody would notice.

The unfortunate dreg, the real Webley, had, once again, been sent to Limbo.

Alfa noticed that Webley was missing, but he then suddenly appeared, clutching his bottle of Medicine.

Everyone was asked by Alfa to commence their search, stating that there should be another clue, within the Theatre.

Hermes asked Alfa to accompany Dame and Dombey to the upper part of the Theatre and confirmed that both he and Webley would search the lower parts. The old professor also confirmed that he and Alfa would remain telepathically linked, should anything be found, and everyone understood.

Dame showed Dombey and Alfa the way to the Upper Gallery; Dombey spotted the stage from the high level and said he would love to attend a performance one day. Dame was delighted, and suggested that he give her a call. Dombey's face started to redden after Dame's comments.

They arrived at the top of the Theatre to begin their search; Alfa checked the walls and ceilings, Dombey looked under the seats, and Dame asked what they were actually searching for, as she told them, she knew every inch of the Theatre.

Alfa could only confirm that they were looking for something unusual.

Korpos impatiently watched the events going on at the Theatre, and Malus had asked him to assist Asper, if there were any problems.

The evil Jinn Soldier was angry over his master not asking him to reveal his plans, as he wanted to gain recognition for his abilities.

'I will show Malus that I, Korpos, is the best Warrior of the Jinn Army!'

Hermes and Webley searched the dressing rooms, then Webley asked his master about what they were actually searching for.

The old professor explained that the clue from the paperweight had led them to the Theatre, and that they should look carefully for anything unusual, something that felt it did not belong there.

Hermes sensed that the Jinn were close by, and warned Webley to be careful, as they were being watched. The Jinn warrior silently laughed, from inside Webley's body.

Korpos grew tired of waiting, as he watched the three dregs below him. He decided to drift down to the lower parts of the Theatre, as he wanted to see whether the other two dregs were having any better luck.

Hermes was searching the Gift Shop and asked Webley to help him. He pointed to the paperweights, confirming that they were similar to the one that Alfa had found, so Webley looked at the glass objects closely.

Hermes senses were telling him that the Jinn were closing in, but he could only see Webley, then an invisible Korpos entered the theatre gift shop.

Asper could not say or do anything to jeopardise his position inside Webley's body, and remained silent.

Hermes picked up a Theatre Programme and looked at the cover with interest. He knew there was danger close by, and quietly slipped the programme into a large pocket, inside his coat.

'Webley, said the old wizard, keep searching here for the moment, I must make sure the others are alright!'

He left the Gift Shop and made his way to the Main Stairs. He telepathically contacted Alfa, and asked him to meet him in the Gift Shop, stating that they had unwelcome guests!

Webley was interrupted by the return of the old Wizard, who now had Alfa at his side.

'Have you managed to find anything Webley? '

'No Sir, nothing at all' replied the startled small dreg!

Hermes was convinced that there was something strange about Webley's manner.

Alfa too, sensed the presence of the Jinn.

Webley picked up a smiling Theatrical Masque from a display cabinet and placed it over his face.

Hermes then knew that this was not the real Webley, and telepathically spoke to Alfa, who concurred.

Korpos watched the small dreg hiding behind the Masque and made him disappear.

A glowing Masque then fell to the floor.

Hermes and Alfa looked around, but saw nothing except for the Masque and assumed that another Jinn warrior was present, but invisible, except that Alfa saw a transparent shape, a shape that he had seen before.

'Yes, dreg, it is I, Korpos'. Your puny friend is now in the place we met before; he is in the Bastille of Pain!'

Korpos told them, that he had transported Webley to the place of punishment for the Jinn, and stated that he was now going to capture everyone.

Hermes and Alfa transported themselves to the upper gallery, and found that Korpos was already there.

The evil Jinn warrior was hovering over Dame and Dombey, the professor and his apprentice were too late!

Hermes raised his webbed hands, trying to stop the Jinn warrior, by sending both his cousin and Dombey to a safe place, then a small figure appeared, who looked very frightened and was visibly shaking.

Webley had returned, but was in a state of shock!

Korpos couldn't believe his evil eyes. *'I sent you to the Bastille, how were you able to return?'*

Hermes then realised that Webley's body had been taken over by the Jinn and had been sent to the Jinn prison, but Korpos had wrongly sent Asper to the Bastille, causing the real Webley to return safely.

Alfa picked up the glowing Masque and threw it at the shape of Korpos, causing the evil disciple to vanish straight away.

Hermes returned Dame and Dombey from their safe refuge, and explained to his bewildered allies over the Jinn's incompetence with Webley's body.

'It was Asper that took over Webley's body, explained Hermes. He was sent to the Bastille of Pain by Korpos, who was unaware he was actually sending another Jinn there!'

Webley was still in shock, and shaking!

'They are certainly using more and more devious methods, exclaimed Hermes; and as we are much closer to our quest, I can only reiterate that we must be more careful, and *extremely* vigilant!!'

Webley stated that the he'd been sent to Limbo, by the Jinn warrior, which was a terrible place to be in, and was glad to have returned. He then asked the old wizard of how the Masque had vanished.

'When Korpos made you disappear, stated the wise old wizard, the Masque absorbed some of his powers, but remained here, so we used these remaining powers to turn the tables, resulting in his failure!'

Dombey placed his arm over his small friend's shoulder and welcomed him back to safety, stressing that he was safe once more.

Hermes checked to see that the Theatre Programme was safe inside his pocket and called to everyone, stating that they still had some work to do, as they had finished at the Theatre.

Hermes asked Alfa to join him back at Russell Square and asked Dombey and Webley to stay on with his cousin, Dame, confirming that they would be well looked after by his cousin.

'I am sorry cousin, that you and Alfa cannot stay, said Dame, but I understand, and will make Dombey and Webley welcome'.

'You are an incompetent fool Korpos, go, go back to the Bastille, I do not want to see you for a long time, maybe never!' Shouted the Prince of Curses.

Korpos tried to explain to his master, but vanished before he could speak!

Asper entered the chamber.

'I am giving you a second chance Asper, go back to the Theatre and bring me the dreg called Dame, and do not fail me!'

The evil mercenary materialised outside the room below the stage, where Dame was entertaining her two guests with tea and cakes. She noticed that Dombey had a very large appetite and told them she would go and get some more food.

As she entered her small room, an unwelcome visitor stood behind her.

Dombey called out to Dame, and asked if she wanted any help, but heard no reply. He went over to the adjoining room and spotted a broken plate, and all the cakes, which were scattered over the floor.

'Webley, we must get to Hermes and Alfa, Dame has been captured by the Jinn!'

The two dregs hurried through the tunnels and gulley's, as fast as they could.

Hermes produced the Theatre programme from his inside coat pocket and asked Alfa to take a look at the picture on the front cover. Alfa studied the glossy picture while the old Wizard went off to get a chart.

'It is all beginning to make sense now, the two metal girders were part of a structure,' Alfa stated with excitement.

The structure in the picture was of Tower Bridge, with a large ship passing through. The bridge was in the open position, and the two iron beams were pointing at the overhead tunnel, between the two towers.

'This is where we will find the lost book Alfa, stated the old Professor, here, take a look at the chart!'

Alfa was relieved that they were so close to the book, but the old wizard looked puzzled and informed Alfa that there was a possible snag.

'The chart reveals that any missing object will appear, only for a brief moment in time, but we need to check on how long, seconds, minutes, hours; I cannot confirm how long, but it does tell us that the object will appear in two days from now, so we need to start planning, so that we are prepared and ready for the return of our book!'

Alfa checked the chart, hoping to find more clues!

The Professor confirmed that they had some more research to do, as it was imperative to get this exactly right, and that it was probably their only chance to retrieve the lost book.

'Come my boy, let us get some rest, we need to be ready for our final part of the quest.'

Alfa confirmed that he was very tired and was given a pillow by Hermes, inviting him to lay down on a mattress, within the secret room.

Alfa went to sleep straight away. His mind was focussed on Tower Bridge and hopefully, getting back the book of dreg civilisation.

'So, you are the dreg they call Dame,' roared Malus!

Dame was very frightened, as she stood before Malus and Asper, who both laughed when she screamed for help!

'Scream as loud as you wish, your friends cannot hear you in our dark lands!'

Dame felt helpless and wished she was back in the Theatre.

Hermes was in a deep sleep, but was awoken by the arrival of Dombey and Webley.

The two dregs had returned to Russell Square as quickly as they could and were exhausted.

Dombey was still out of breath and the Professor asked him what was wrong.

'They have taken Dame, shouted Dombey. The Jinn have captured Dame, while we were having tea at the Theatre. We searched for her, but saw a smashed plate and cakes all over the floor; she just vanished!'

'Oh dear, the old Wizard exclaimed, poor Dame!'

Alfa heard the commotion and asked what had happened.

The Professor confirmed the situation and knew the Jinn would want something in return for the release of his cousin.

He asked Dombey and Webley to wait outside the secret room, knowing that they would both understand.

'So, my young apprentice, the Jinn will require something for Dame's return, and we will give them some clues, but not necessarily the correct clues!'

Alfa gave the old wizard a puzzled look?

'We will send them to the Tower, but not the Bridge, we will give them the details, and let them go to the "Tower of London", which will hopefully, give us enough time to collect the book.'

Alfa agreed that this was a great idea, but asked his master about the timing, as they only had a small "window" of opportunity, when the book would appear.

Hermes knew that time was important, and said they would need to go to the Tower of London the next day, so that they would not have too far to travel, the day after.

'Now, everyone, get some rest please,' called Hermes.

He gave Dombey and Webley some bedding and asked them to make themselves comfortable.

He told them that they would be going on a very important assignment the next day, and that they should get as much sleep as possible.

The old Professor returned to his sleeping quarters and thought about what they could do, to fool the Jinn once again, but more importantly, to get Dame back, safely.

'I must not fail Dame, muttered the old wizard; she will be scared, and is depending on me!'

He started to snore and drifted back into a deep sleep,

once again.

Both rooms were very quiet, with the exception of the snoring Professor; as everyone was also, fast asleep!

Each of the dregs were dreaming about a plan to safely get Dame back.

Dame concentrated and sent her thoughts over to Hermes, hoping the telepathy would work and wishing she had spent more time listening to her cousin, when he tried to teach her the powers.

Alfa was picking up Dames thought waves and knew she was alright.

He could not make contact with her, as this may have placed her in danger.

14: A CONFLICT AT TOWER BRIDGE.

The next day was bright and sunny, the great River Thames looked quite clear for a change and reflected the warm rays, of the sun.

There was not one cloud in the sky, and the City of London looked like a scene from a picture Postcard.

The cobbled pathways surrounded the majestic Castle, which were full of tourists, from all over the world, each holding tightly onto their guide maps and each having a desire to learn more about England's amazing History.

The Tower of London was an awesome sight; one of the Queens Bodyguards, a Yeoman of the Guard, stood by one of the many gates.

The guard was dressed in his bright red and gold knee-length Tunic, with a sash across his left shoulder and a white Ruff around his neck.

To finish off his unique look, he wore a black round cap with a brim, and a red band.

The sun was shining over the huge bridge, viewed from Tower Hill, with its twin towers and connecting structure above. The bridge was built to allow vehicles to pass over it, to access other parts of the city, or to the South of London, when travelling the opposite way. The river Thames flowed quietly below, with small crafts passing underneath.

Tower Bridge was the real venue for Alfa, whose task was to retrieve the Lost "Book of Dreg civilisation", which would appear somewhere within the famous twin-towered building, at a given time period, hopefully, before the Jinn had found out their plans.

The only other clue he had, was that the lost book would appear, once the bridge had fully lifted its "splitting" road.

Alfa had a busy day ahead of him; somehow, he had to get Dombey and Webley into the Tower of London and, once they were safe inside, he would then be able to get over to Tower Bridge, and wait for it to fully open.

Dame, the cousin of the old professor, was imprisoned in the "Bloody Tower", by the evil Jinn, who had agreed to release her, subject to being given more details about the book, when they were told to go to the tower.

Back in Russell Square, Alfa was preparing his final plans for Dombey and Webley, with Hermes listening carefully, so that he could advise, but also, to ensure that his cousin Dame was safely released.

Hermes also looked closely at an Astrological Chart in meticulous detail; every effort had to be made, as timing was of paramount importance, if they wanted to succeed with their final quest.

Alfa sat in silence and Hermes looked over at his troubled colleague.

'I know what you're thinking my boy, but don't

worry, we will get my cousin back!'

Alfa's concentration was broken, and agreed with his master.

Dombey and Webley were eating breakfast, but they too, were also thinking about Dame.

'When should we go to the Tower of London Professor', asked Dombey?

Hermes asked him to be patient and confirmed that they would all need to finalise any plans, before they left Russell Square.

The four of them entered the old wizard's secret, soundproofed room.

Dombey had managed to grab a handful of fruit, on his way in, and Webley picked up his medicine bottle, then gulped a very large dose of the tincture.

The old professor laid out several Astrological Charts on the floor and pinned another one, onto the wall.

'This chart gives us the exact location of our good book', stated the old wizard.

Hermes had pointed to a cluster of stars with a baton and continued.

'This constellation tells me that the object will appear sometime tomorrow, over the rising bridge!'

Alfa picked up a similar chart, to check on his master's prophecies and noticed something was wrong.

'Professor, said Alfa, look at this chart I have here, I sense a problem!'

Hermes glanced at the duplicate chart and looked puzzled.

'This chart is very similar, to the one on the wall, but there is something wrong with your calculations!' Exclaimed Alfa.

Hermes placed the second chart up against the other chart, and noticed that there was a Ginger Beer stain on it. He checked the chart and gasped!

Dombey and Webley looked embarrassed, but kept quiet.

'If these details are correct my friends, said the old professor, we have no time to lose. The stain has covered an important time zone and my calculations were one day out; the Bridge will open sometime later today!'

Alfa knew that timing was now, very important, and made is way quickly towards the door.

He asked Hermes to explain the plans for Dame's rescue with Dombey and Webley, and that he was on his way to Tower Bridge.

The old professor started to panic, but confirmed that he would be in contact, by telepathy. He warned Alfa not to open the lost book if he managed to retrieve it, as he would need to release a spell from it.

Alfa confirmed he had understood and finally left.

Hermes now had to think of a plan, as time was running out for Dame.

The Bloody Tower stood out from the surrounding buildings inside the confines of the Tower of London, it was very dark and musty inside the small cell where Dame was being kept, against her will.

Many centuries ago, the "Bloody Tower" was used as a prison, to hold various people, including Royalty, who awaited their punishment for the crimes they had allegedly committed.

A spiral staircase in the tower, led to the upper rooms and the Dungeons.

One of the Dungeons was inhabited by two figures

and a Black Horse.

Dame was chained to a wall, and beside her was the Horse's Master, Tavet!

Malus had sent them to the Dungeon, as part of his cunning plan, to get the lost book into the Jinn's possession, somehow, before the dregs could obtain it.

Tavet was instructed not to release the prisoner, until he was given something in exchange for her.

Tavet knew that failure again, would result in a *very* harsh penalty from the "Prince of Curses".

'I will not fail you this time my Lord'! Exclaimed Tavet.

These were the words of a desperate Demon!

Alfa arrived at Tower Bridge and was in awe of the wonderful construction, which had been built in 1886, over an eight-year period.

Within the walls of the tower, were the amazing Crown Jewels, which could be inspected by the public, by taking a "Travelator"; a moving walk-way, placed each side of the exhibits.

Alfa wondered where to begin his search, then found the stairs in one of the twin-towers.

He started to climb the endless number of steps before him, and sensed that there was no evil presence for a change.

He then entered the overhead walkway, that was connected to the second tower.

He looked out of the glass windows and spotted the Tower of London in the distance, hoping that Dame was safe and unharmed.

Hermes transported himself, Dombey and Webley to the Tower of London, to save valuable time and made their way carefully to the "Bloody Tower".

'There was no time to think about a plan of action,' mumbled Hermes.

'I had to make a "spur of the moment" reaction, he confirmed; and hope things will be in our favour!'

They ascended the spiral staircase towards the Bloody Tower, not aware that they were being watched by Malus.

Malus could only see three dregs and wondered where the young boy was.

He knew they were up to something, so he scanned the rest of the Tower, to see if he was near; his senses told him that he was close by.

Alfa continued with his search, this time in the other tower, but still, he couldn't find anything.

All he could do was wait for the bridge to open.

He looked both ways across the river Thames, but couldn't see any large vessels making their way towards the Bridge.

Tavet sensed he had company and checked the chains holding Dame. He made them tighter, then backed his horse into the shadows.

Hermes had heard the chains rattle and asked his two companions to be on their guard.

Webley gulped a large dose of his medicine and Dombey rolled up his shirtsleeves.

The door to the dungeon was locked, so Hermes produced a small bottle of green liquid, then called out!

'Release the prisoner, or face the consequences!'

Tavet laughed and invited them to come and get her.

Hermes asked his two friends to stand back, then splashed some of the green liquid over the dungeon door, which caused a small explosion and the lock to vanish.

They entered the cell and Dame expressed her gratitude to them, for coming to her rescue.

Tavet trotted forward, but his mount was quite shaken by the blast.

The horse started to rear and they saw his nostrils beginning to emit some smoke; he was getting ready to snort flames!

'I believe you have something for me Professor' said Tavet!

'Let her go and I will give you what you ask', replied Hermes.

'No old man, you will need to give me something first, then I will release her to you!'

The black horse's front legs were now above the old wizard.

'As you wish evil one, there, now look over to the wall and take what you see, then you shall release the lady!'

Tavet saw a bright halo on the wall, which surrounded a scroll, a vision that he had heard of, from his master, Malus.

Hermes explained that the scroll would tell him the location of the lost book.

Tavet asked him to pass him the scroll and then he would release his prisoner.

Both Dombey and Webley looked on in amazement, wondering why the old Professor would give such a revealing clue to the Jinn.

Hermes reached out and removed the scroll from the vision, then passed it over to the evil Horseman.

As he snatched the parchment, the chains holding

Dame fell to the floor.

Dombey grabbed Dame and lifted her up and led her away from her prison cell.

Hermes checked, to make sure that his cousin was alright, and asked them all to depart as quickly as possible, so that they could join Alfa.

The young dreg was sitting cross-legged inside the overhead walkway above the Bridge, waiting patiently for the Bridge to open.

His master had telepathically informed him, that Dame had been released safely.

Malus greeted Tavet with apprehension, and waited for his evil Horseman to pass him the scroll, so that he could see what was on it.

'So Tavet, it appears we have the location of the "Book of Dreg Civilisation"; now we have work to do. You will ask Asper to return, so that we can plan our next move!'

A very pleased but ugly horseman summoned Asper as commanded.

Malus confirmed that they were going to Tower Bridge and that this is where the book will be.

He thought to himself that this was too easy and that they must be up to their tricks again.

He angrily slammed his fist down, onto a table and shouted.

'They have tricked us, he shouted. The scroll states that the book was sent to "The Zone of Light", earlier this morning, but their book was lost some time ago'!

He then ordered his soldiers to meet him at the Bridge.

Hermes asked Webley to escort Dame back to Drury Lane, and bade farewell to his cousin, who wished them all good luck in their quest, for the book.

Hermes and Dombey left the Tower of London and made their way through the tunnels and gullies, for the short journey, across to Tower Bridge.

Tower Bridge stood motionless, overlooking the grand river Thames.

There was no sign of movement when they entered one of the twin towers, but Alfa had already sensed their presence below.

The old Professor discussed the "Decoy" scroll with Alfa and wondered how long it would be, before the Jinn knew they had been tricked.

Alfa's concentration was suddenly broken by a familiar sound, he could hear the faint sound of hooves, which became louder and louder.

In the distance he spotted the silhouette of a Horse and Rider.

It's Tavet,' confirmed Alfa!

Alfa warned everyone to be careful, but they had already found their way to the overhead span.

'It appears that Malus himself, has also come to the Bridge, stated Hermes; he is not alone, he brings with him Tavet, the evil Horseman, so he is obviously annoyed at being tricked once again. So, gentlemen, it is time we prepare ourselves for a battle!'

The wise old Wizard held his arms out and waggled his fingers in the air. Alfa copied his master and concentrated on the roof of the walkway. Dombey was watching the evil Horseman getting closer to them.

A cloud of smoke appeared, which was surrounding a

shiny object; the "Sword of Truth"!

Alfa pulled the sword out of the mist and clutched it, very tightly.

Malus spotted the sword and remembered its mighty powers he had witnessed, on the Tree Walk, at Battersea Park, and reacted immediately!

'Lord of the night, I call upon thee to grant me the power of your mightiness!'

Hermes and Alfa both shuddered over the words spoken by the evil Jinn master, who was invisible.

'Brother Cerberus, I ask that you send to me, the "Weapon of Death", send to me your mighty sword!'

A small dot appeared and "zig-zagged" its way over to Malus.

The dot started to grow larger and circled its way over to the hand of the prince of curses. Malus, and a sword suddenly became visible!

'Behold dreg infidel's, roared Malus. I too have a mighty weapon of great strength, and beware, this is the "Sword of Cerberus", which I will use to defeat you!'

Malus held the sword high; its shiny blade reflected the sun and dazzled the onlooking dregs.

Hermes had seen this sword before, many years ago and wondered whether it was any match for their weapon.

Alfa prepared himself for the inevitable clash with the Jinn Master.

Hermes asked Dombey to join him, and passed him a small phial, then explained it would slow down the enemy when used. He warned him to use it very carefully, and to place a small drop in his hand when required, then to blow it into the face of any Jinn members. Dombey placed the small phial into his pocket, checked it was secure and hid behind a pillar.

The aging wizard confirmed to Alfa that he was too old for fighting and that he would be his strength.

Alfa raised his sword, then kissed the handle and shouted.

'For all of the dregs!'

Tavet pulled the reins tight, his steed raised his front legs high, and snorted two jets of fire.

Asper blended into the overhead timber joists and concentrated his thoughts on Dombey.

Malus called out to Hermes.

'So, you send a young boy to do battle with I, the Prince of Curses!'

Hermes glanced at the sword Malus was holding, once again, and warned Alfa that the weapon was indeed very powerful and, that should it touch anyone or anything, that they, or it would turn to dust!

Alfa shuddered at the thought, but confirmed that he would continue, for the sake of every dreg.

Hermes did assure him, that his blade would not be affected.

Malus moved closer to Alfa; Hermes moved aside.

Dombey could see a strange shape hovering above him and knew it must be Asper.

Dombey couldn't reveal himself, so had to wait for his chance to attack.

Tavet then raced towards Hermes, holding a red lance under his arm.

Alfa touched swords with Malus, the noise from the two metal shafts echoed throughout the bridge, causing each of the dregs, to cover their ears.

The two foes continued fighting and lunging at each other, as flashes of lightning started to appear from the evil Jinn's blade.

Malus was very strong thought Alfa, but he knew he had youth, and speed to his advantage.

'Your master taught you well young dreg, but be prepared to suffer defeat!'

Malus lunged at Alfa and narrowly missed his side; the old professor had to do something; he couldn't allow his young apprentice be defeated.

Hermes was helpless, he was pinned to the side of the walkway, by the lance, which was held by Tavet!

The old wizard summoned all the strength he could muster and managed to push aside the red lance; he then ducked below the horse and ran over to Dombey.

'Quick Dombey, throw me the phial!' Shouted Hermes.

Hermes placed a small drop onto his hand and threw the bottle back to Dombey. He blew hard on his webbed hand, and the charging horseman stopped in his tracks, both he and his horse were turned into ice!

The sword fight was still ongoing. Asper hovered over the ice statue of his Jinn brother, without noticing Dombey at his side.

Another ice statue appeared; Asper too, was frozen!

'Well done, Dombey' called Hermes!

Hermes and Dombey both hurried over to Alfa and Malus, but the Jinn master backed away from the young boy, and raised his sword at the ice statues.

A shaft of light freed the evil horseman and Asper.

Dombey quickly blew another drop of the green liquid

over to Tavet, who once again became frozen; he also used the opportunity to break the red lance.

Asper revealed his hideous form and made his way over to Hermes, but Dombey realised what was going on and blew some liquid over Asper, again, he became a solid lump of ice.

Malus tried to push Alfa into a corner, so that he could free his two frozen soldiers at the same time.

Dombey caught him off guard and blew some liquid at him. Now there were three ice statues!

Hermes congratulated Dombey on his outstanding bravery, and suggested they move away from the scene, as he was not sure how long the ice spell would last for.

Dombey then confirmed that a large ship was coming towards the bridge! He shouted that there was a large vessel, looking as though it was on a collision course.

Then they heard the sound of heavy machinery within the towers.

Alfa looked below and saw that the bridge had started to split in its centre, with the road now slowly raising itself, towards the overhead walkway.

Hermes asked Dombey to watch the ice Jinn statues and to use the liquid again, if they looked like any of them were thawing out.

The old wizard was sure it would last for at least, ten or fifteen minutes, but did not want to take any chances.

The machinery within the huge bridge started to raise its two steel channels, that had been used to convey the road traffic, ten minutes before.

A large ship drew closer, waiting for the two channels to be fully raised.

Hermes confirmed to Alfa, that they only had thirty

seconds to retrieve the book, once it had appeared, and, if they failed, it would be another two, or more years, before it would reappear.

Dombey was keeping an eye on the three ice warriors and didn't notice Malus gradually thawing out, who was starting to lift the "Sword of Cerberus".

Dombey jumped as the sword sliced through the broken section of the red lance, as if it were butter.

Dombey had dropped the phial during the commotion, which sprayed the liquid over the helpless dreg, turning *him* into an ice statue, and leaving him with a very pained expression.

The bridge had fully opened, the long ship had started to sail through the temporary opening. A Bright star then appeared at the centre of the two beams, between the two towers.

'It's the book master,' shouted Alfa!

Alfa passed the Sword of Truth to the old wizard and ran over to the star, to retrieve the lost tome; the lost book had returned!

Malus crept up behind Hermes and pushed his sword into the old Professor, which left, just a pile of dust heaped up, on the surface, with the sword of truth, lying next to the pile.

'HERMES'!!!!

Alfa's cries filled the tower, then a sudden darkness filled the air.

Malus pointed his sword at Alfa, who stated that the Jinn would never possess the book, and quickly threw the book into the air.

The Jinn master levitated himself towards the spot, but the book had vanished into thin air.

Alfa concentrated on the Sword of Truth, which had magically appeared in his hand.

Tavet appeared out of his frozen form and charged over to Alfa, picking up the broken lance on his way.

Alfa raised the sword of truth, and made circles at the oncoming rider.

The evil horseman stopped in his tracks. He then ran over to Dombey and released him from his frozen state.

The young dreg made sure his friend was okay and passed him a mirror, knowing that Asper was nearby, and, that he knew exactly what to do with it.

Alfa turned to face Malus once again.

'Your old master has gone now dreg; it is time for you to join him!'

Once again, the two enemies were fighting with their steel weapons.

Alfa seemed to be gaining extra strength

Dombey looked at the remains of Hermes and sighed. He then called out to Asper to show himself, as he wanted revenge for the death of Hermes.

The hideous form of the Jinn soldier appeared, Dombey had averted his eyes, but felt them wanting to gaze on the Jinn soldier.

Suddenly, Asper vanished; Dombey had placed the mirror over his eyes and Asper had been looking, at his own reflection!

Malus and Alfa were still in battle, with flashes of lightning filling the room.

Dombey still had part of the broken lance with him and ran over to assist his friend.

He waited for the right moment and shouted at Alfa to step aside, then threw the lance towards Malus.

The lance shattered one of the windows of the overhead walkway; a strong gust of wind then blew through, causing the ashes of Hermes to surround Malus.

A loud scream was heard, Malus and the sword of Cerberus had vanished.

Dombey picked up the remaining ashes of the old professor and pulled a handkerchief from his pocket.

He neatly tied the piece of cotton cloth and placed it into his pocket.

'We will return to Russell Square and consult the Elders; they will advise us, said Alfa!'

Dombey followed Alfa down the steps, then back to the lower parts of the bridge. They heard the two steel channels slowly returning to their original position; the impatient motorists then continued with their journeys.

It was a very sad meeting at Russell Square; the elders of all the dreg tribes had gathered to pay their respects to the late Hermes.

The remaining ashes of the old professor were poured from the handkerchief, into a glass jar, then taken to his secret chamber.

The gathered dregs stood in silence as Alfa spoke of his late master.

'He gave his own life to save mine, sighed Alfa, for that I will be eternally grateful!'

Rank moved one pace forward, clicked his heels and saluted the remains of his dear friend.

Slooth laid his magnifying glass by the ashes.

Uncle Wadd bowed his head, then touched the jar and muttered something about meeting soon.

Dombey and Webley could do nothing except stare at

the remains.

Everyone except Alfa and Dame left the secret room, and went into the adjoining room for some refreshments.

Alfa comforted Dame, as she laid some flowers at the side of her cousin's ashes, in the room.

'Alfa, I sense that something more than the death of Hermes is troubling you?'

Dame's powers seemed to be getting stronger, since the loss of her cousin.

Alfa pointed to a book on the shelf behind Dame.

'It's the Book of…!'

Alfa put a finger to his lips.

Dame asked him how he had managed to get the book away from the Jinn.

Alfa responded, stating that he had sent it to the only place the Jinn could not penetrate; the secret room of Hermes.

'In this book, said Alfa, there are many secrets and maybe there will be a way to bring back Hermes, but we cannot open the book yet, as Hermes had stated that a spell had to be released first!'

Dame suggested that Alfa should consult uncle Wadd, as he would be the one who would know how to release the spell from the book.

They both left the secret room and joined the other mourners in the next room.

Float and Levi were in deep conversation with Snak, reminiscing about the adventures they had together, in the quest for the book.

A lonely figure had entered the secret room and had his head bowed.

Buck was feeling guilty over his greed, at the Old

Bailey, as he stared at the ashes.

Alfa spotted Buck and went over to console him, confirming that at some stage, we all make mistakes and that Hermes had already forgiven him.

Some of the guests were starting to leave and Alfa asked if Rank and uncle Wadd could stay for a while.

Dombey ushered the departing dregs toward the nearest tunnels and asked if Webley could guard the door to the secret room and not to let anyone in.

Rank and Uncle Wadd were seated at the table, Alfa placed a book by the side of the ashes containing Hermes.

'So, said Wadd, you have managed to retrieve the lost book my boy, well done, well done!'

Uncle Wadd was somehow not surprised!

Wadd touched the leather-bound manuscript and asked if the spell had been broken.

Alfa explained that Hermes had had no time, before he was slain by Malus.

Uncle Wadd picked up the book and placed it into an empty space on the top shelf, then asked Rank to remove it.

Rank complied with the instructions.

'Alfa, now you must replace the book'.

He did as he was told.

Uncle Wadd then turned to Dame and asked her to remove the book and place it on the table.

As she did, a green glow surrounded it and the clasp holding the book together, opened.

Uncle Wadd then picked up the book and opened it.

'Return my lord Hermes, return from your sleep, oh wise wizard of the dregs!'

A thin shaft of light appeared over the glass jar; then the lid started to unscrew itself.

Hermes stood beside Alfa, Rank stood to attention and saluted the return of the old Professor.

Hermes congratulated Alfa for returning the book to the secret room.

Dame looked at her cousin and wiped away a tear from her face.

Dombey and Webley had heard the commotion inside the secret room and entered.

They looked across and saw Hermes, and both their jaws dropped.

'Welcome back Sir, called Dombey, but how was this possible?'

'All in good time my friends, all in good time!'

Hermes told his guests that he would need to return the book, back to the Zone of Light, straight away; where the Jinn would not be able to find it.

'The Jinn will not rest until they have this special book,' said the wise old professor!

As the jubilant dregs discussed their victory at Tower Bridge, a gloomy atmosphere surrounded the Jinn Empire, in the dark lands of Inferus.

'One day, we will return, stated the Prince of Curses!'

Malus and his evil disciples were already plotting their revenge.

Is this the End; or is this just the beginning?

Printed in Great Britain
by Amazon